PROSOPAGNOSIA

PROSOP

GNOSIA

SÒNIA HERNÁNDEZ

TRANSLATED FROM THE SPANISH
BY SAMUEL RUTTER

SCRIBE

Melbourne • London

Scribe Publications
2 John St, Clerkenwell, London, WC1N 2ES, United Kingdom
18–20 Edward St, Brunswick, Victoria 3056, Australia
3754 Pleasant Ave, Suite 100, Minneapolis, Minnesota 55409, USA

First published in Spanish as *El hombre que se creía Vicente Rojo*

First published by Scribe 2021

Typeset in Portrait Text by the publishers

Printed and bound in the UK by CPI Group (UK) Ltd,
Croydon CR0 4YY

Scribe Publications is committed to the sustainable use of natural
resources and the use of paper products made responsibly from
those resources.

978 1 912854 77 6 (UK edition)
978 1 950354 44 3 (US edition)
978 1 925849 72 1 (Australian edition)
978 1 9259383 9 5 (ebook)

Catalogue records for this book are available from the National
Library of Australia and the British Library.

This project has been assisted by the Australian government
through the Australia Council for the Arts, its arts funding
and advisory body.

scribepublications.co.uk
scribepublications.com
scribepublications.com.au

PART 1

PROSOPAGNOSIA

Berta says that beautiful things aren't made for her, or that she isn't destined to have them, or that the only things she deserves are ugly. Scientific studies have shown that memory is constructed the same way a story is put together: sentences impose order on a series of images, experiences, and feelings to create a plot. And memory is fundamental to the creation of identity. Berta insists that she cannot have anything beautiful, nor can anything beautiful happen to her. Because she has already passed judgement on her life, she is able to understand her reality in precisely those terms.

Berta is fifteen years old. A few months ago, she bought clippers, which she used to shave off practically all her hair. She says that this way, it's easier to imagine the skull hidden beneath her stubbly scalp. It's the only part of her body that she exhibits with anything like pleasure, and not exactly because she likes it, or is proud of it. She feels a deep sense of aversion for her whole body, in fact, which is why she hides it under baggy jeans and woollen jumpers. It's difficult to imagine a teenage body under there.

Sometimes she locks herself in the bathroom and stares fixedly at her own reflection in the mirror. This is one of the main ways she spends her time. Despite how this may seem, she doesn't do it in order to recognise herself, nor is she poring over every inch of her skin in search of some clue that would reveal bodily signs of life. Quite the opposite. She stands in front of the mirror, forcing herself not to blink until her eyes see only an image in which it is impossible to discern the necessary harmony or balance to compose a face.

One of her teachers explained, in class, an illness called 'prosopagnosia', which is the inability to recognise faces. Berta feels an uncanny sense of satisfaction when she arrives at the point where she no longer recognises her reflection in the mirror. Through this dissociation, she manages to see herself from the outside, as if she were a different person, but without a body. Someone observing a mass of matter without meaning or purpose.

The teacher in question was supposed to be giving an introductory class on psychology, and he thought he would capture the students' attention by beginning with perception and all the illusions the human brain is capable of creating. He spent a good number of hours drawing cubes on the blackboard, which he then used to demonstrate the mutability of a geometric figure that in the first dimension was just a square. But depending on how you looked at it, it seemed able to pass into the second dimension. By the same token, sometimes the cube seemed to be angled to the left, while at others times it was angled to the right. Even though it was the very same figure, depending on the perspective, you could view the cube either from above or from below.

Just as the teacher had hoped, the students were fascinated by the class. Berta was fascinated too, because she liked the idea that the forms we perceive as perfect can be broken down into less harmonious forms, if we are able to banish from our brains the received notions that tell us how we should interpret the final object. In some ways, the teacher's scientific reasoning proved her right, because if reality isn't manipulated during the process of perception by the words that adults force us to learn, it is, as a consequence, always less balanced and empty of meaning.

One day she was on the cusp of passing out in the bathroom while she stared at herself in the mirror. She held her eyes open as wide as she could, in order to see from *behind* them, to see directly with her brain. Without realising it, she'd stopped breathing, and she only began to do so again when she noticed the first signs of fainting. But those instincts didn't kick in the next time, when she was in the entrance hall of her high school. She would have hit her head hard against the floor or the wall if it hadn't been for a stranger who happened to be standing nearby at the moment she passed out. This time it hadn't happened in the bathroom, but right in front of the receptionist's desk by the school's entrance. Someone had left a large painting leaning against the wall; its entire surface was covered in colourful geometric combinations that created different visual effects with depth and perspective. There were stairways made of different colours where it was impossible to tell if the stairs went up or down. Perhaps they weren't stairs at all, but buildings wedged close together, sharing walls. Straightaway, Berta thought of the cube her psychology teacher had drawn on the blackboard. She stopped in front of the painting and tried to distinguish the different levels of overlapping figures and the variable depths in the canvas. She probably also stopped breathing.

She came to surrounded by teachers, the receptionist, and (although she couldn't have known in that moment) the man who had caught her at just the right moment and stopped her from bashing her head. Berta didn't want them to call her mother, and in the end they all agreed that it was nothing more than a dizzy spell. The man, whom Berta had never met before, offered to walk her home, because he lived nearby. Once again, the teachers and the receptionist agreed that this was the best course of action.

Along the way, the man told her that he had been watching her while she was staring at the painting. She was feeling rather ashamed about everything that had happened and for the fuss she had caused at school. Luckily, it had occurred at a time when there was barely anyone around. But the man made her feel protected and ashamed in equal measures, perhaps because it had already been made clear to her that she ought to be grateful to him. The man gave off a metallic smell. He wasn't much taller than her, with a pointed, greying beard. She felt so uncomfortable that she even began to regret not letting the teachers call her mother. Awkward things always happened to her.

'Do you like the painting? Was there something in particular that you were looking at with such concentration?'

She didn't feel like talking with this man at all, but the silence was even more unbearable.

'I don't know.'

'If you like it, it's yours.'

The old man's comment made Berta laugh. She broke out in a nervous laughter that embarrassed her even more, because she didn't know exactly what she was laughing about. While they walked, she listened to the man's breathing. She wanted to get home as soon as possible. She told him he didn't need to accompany her, that for some time now she had made her own way to and from school, and that she was in a hurry. But he just told her that he would feel better, having witnessed her fainting spell, if he saw her arrive home safe and sound. He spoke in a low, calm voice, with a peculiar accent that Berta couldn't identify.

He told her that if she preferred, they didn't have to speak, or even walk together. He would walk a few steps behind her, close enough to make sure that everything was okay, but not so close that it would bother her. Berta didn't say no, but she didn't feel any better either when the man fell back a few paces for the last stretch before she arrived home. He didn't stand next to her even when she stopped at the traffic lights, and yet Berta knew that he was right there behind her. She didn't even turn around when she reached the front door to her building. In fear, she opened the door, went in, and ran up the stairs to her apartment as quickly as she could.

The next morning, the painting was no longer leaning against the wall in the entrance hall of the high school. Berta didn't want to explain what had happened the day before to Lucas or Mario, and she hoped that none of the teachers who had been there would be so indiscreet as to mention it in front of anyone else. Luckily, they didn't. Even the principal failed to mention it as she came by Berta's desk to drop off a maroon-coloured envelope that Berta left unopened until she arrived home. Shortly after she went through the doors of the high school, standing by a traffic light on a nearby corner she saw the man who had accompanied her yesterday after her dizzy spell. Although their eyes met, neither one of them greeted the other.

The envelope hadn't been manufactured in bulk, that much was clear. Someone with skill and good taste had spent a fair amount of time selecting paper that was sufficiently thick, with a texture that showed the plant fibres and a colour that was vibrant without being shrill. It was a package that announced the value of its contents. Berta left it on the sideboard in the hall. She didn't

7

feel like facing up to whatever it was that the envelope wished to communicate to her. Too many new things had happened in such a short period of time. It was only two months ago that her father had left home, and she thought she had grown used to the new routine, to the changes inflicted upon the stage where her life took place. Her father's voice could no longer be heard at home, and new objects had gradually replaced the ones that used to be there.

When she found out her father was leaving, she didn't seem surprised: perhaps she had already begun to believe that only bad things happened to her. That's also why she didn't believe her father when he tried to make her understand that they were entering a new phase in their lives, in which there would be many subtle improvements and their relationship would grow stronger. From the outset, Berta realised she would have to deal with unpleasant situations, such as the fact that her father's new girlfriend had a deformed arm ending in a stump. A large deformed finger, almost like a hook, jutted out from the stump, with a single ridiculous fingernail painted carefully in a garish shade of red.

On the afternoon the three of them met in a local café, she couldn't get the stump out of her mind while her father was talking. The image of the stump reminded Berta of the exact day she realised she wasn't destined for beautiful things. That day, her kindergarten teacher, Miss Rosa, had been absent from class. The depot-like building that housed her classroom seemed even greyer than usual, despite the colourful drawings covering the walls and windows of the room. Miss Rosa had a daughter whose name Berta found very strange — Zulema, or Zaida, or something like that. Berta hated her, because with a name like that she could feel special, and Berta wanted Miss Rosa's love all for herself. Obviously if Miss Rosa had her own daughter, then she couldn't love Berta all that much, even if she was always the first one to answer the tough questions or to volunteer to clean the blackboard. When Miss Rosa was absent from class, a much older woman came to substitute for her. She wore a dark woollen skirt that reached below her fleshy, lumpy knees but which left her strong calves on display, along with her ankles, which always seemed to be swollen. What's more, she wore huge shoes with long brown shoelaces. These were the sorts of legs Berta's grandmother's friends had, those fat old ladies who were always wrapped up in gowns and florid aprons, scrubbing the stairs. They weren't the legs of a teacher who could help them understand how fun it was to learn the alphabet or draw, so that they could replicate the beautiful objects and nice little animals that made up the world.

Berta also disliked the large, dark jumpers the teacher wore, under which she could sense the enormous sagging breasts that hung down to her waist. She was an old lady, and old ladies shouldn't teach little girls. Her face was round, framed by hair that was wavy without quite being curly, a faded brown with grey roots showing through, hair that she gathered back with a headband. Old women shouldn't use such a childish accessory either. The most repulsive thing about her face was the wart she had on the right side of her mouth. She looked exactly like a witch. It hurt Berta to have this woman as Miss Rosa's substitute teacher.

But it wasn't even the wart sitting on the old woman's hair-shadowed lip that made Berta feel most revolted. The thing she couldn't stand, the thing that made every hair on her body stand on end, was the teacher's undeveloped, deformed hand. It looked like a doll's hand, smaller than normal, incomplete. It would take Berta many years to learn this use of the word *stump*, but that's what it was: a stump with a fleshy hook sticking out of it, and one huge fingernail with a bunch of other stubs a few centimetres long. It was as if someone had mangled the fingers, which in any case could never have grown from such a small hand.

While that witch was in charge of the classroom, Berta never offered to clean the blackboard. The old woman wrote with her left hand and clutched the duster up near her armpit, between her body and her arm, right where that non-hand dangled, a limb far more squalid than the left arm. Berta couldn't stand it. She couldn't look at her. That's also why she couldn't raise her own hand, so young and healthy and well-formed, to answer questions before the others. For many years, she held on to the image of horror that woman conjured in her. A few times, Berta had come across the substitute teacher in the neighbourhood, and she always looked down, hoping she wouldn't recognise her, hoping she wouldn't even see her. On the other hand, she never came across Miss Rosa outside of school, because she lived in a different, much nicer neighbourhood, with her horrible daughter with the strange name, whom she probably took to the park to play with other girls in pretty dresses.

The image of the witch returned powerfully, after so many years, on the afternoon when Berta met with her father and his new girlfriend in a noisy café. By then, she already knew she was obliged to live alongside the ugliest things in the world.

A few days after *that* meeting, the old man appeared and helped her when she was about to pass out at school. The next day, the principal handed her a large envelope that, without a doubt, had something to do with the old man Berta hadn't wanted to acknowledge when she left the school. Too many things to absorb, so the best thing would be to leave it all to one side and dedicate her time to watching how her face breaks down in the mirror's reflection, until it becomes something she no longer recognises, just like how her life had broken down in such a brief period of time. But that afternoon, she was having trouble concentrating. She was trying to look directly with her brain to keep her eyes and her optic nerve from distorting the image she was seeing, but it was complicated. She remembered how difficult it had been in the beginning to see the changes in the cube her teacher had drawn on the board. In fact, she hadn't been able to see the different versions until they had been pointed out to her. She hadn't been able to fully locate the perspective she was looking for in the painting in the entrance hall at school, either. That's when she had the feeling that there was a direct relationship between the painting and the envelope that had been delivered to her by the principal.

The envelope contained a thick piece of paper, and on the blank side you could see the same thick fibres. On the other side, a number of horizontal lines stretched across the surface in a much straighter fashion than some vertical lines of different thicknesses and colours, which were much less firm, and which, on the whole, produced a multitude of irregular squares in warm, ochre tones. Berta searched for the perspective, the mutability of the squares as in the cube drawn by her teacher, but something wasn't right — she couldn't find the perspective, or even a hint of it, like she had been able to with the painting in the entrance hall at school. It wasn't a very good painting. Looking at it properly, you barely had to glance at it before it broke down into the different elements it was made of, because it was nothing more than a jumble of lines and colour that never achieved unity. That's why someone had given it to her; because it was bad. If someone had given her a valuable painting, that would have been surprising.

——

A few days later, they called me at home from the school. My daughter's teacher wished to see me. The call upset me, which is why the teacher, trying to calm me down, said that it was nothing serious, just that some of the other teachers had indicated they were worried about Berta's recent behaviour. When we met in her office at the school, she didn't expand much on what she'd said over the phone. My daughter was often distracted in class, and she had fainted twice. The teachers also believed there was a direct link between Berta's fainting spells and Mario's, who was one of her best friends. That comment seemed very strange to me, but I said I would try to talk to her, although I knew it wouldn't be easy. When I was just about to get up and leave the office, the teacher handed me an envelope that I hadn't noticed until that point. Then she told me that a man who had helped my daughter during one of her fainting spells was also worried about her. He had wanted to give her a painting and she refused to accept it, but he insisted she should have it, and so he'd suggested it could be given to me, even though I'd had no idea about the envelope or the painting until that very moment.

Suddenly, it became clear that the fact that Berta hadn't accepted the man's gift was causing the most conflict, and, apparently, the greatest concern for her teacher. She told me that the man who had done the painting was quite a famous artist, whom the father of one of the students had convinced to give a few talks and art classes after school hours. At the moment, they were considering a project proposed by the artist, along with the catalogues and paintings he had sent in, but the committee hadn't reached a decision yet. It seemed that the art teacher hadn't had her say yet either. In any case, she told me that it was a beautiful painting, and that Berta ought to recognise that it was a friendly gesture. In short, she should accept the gift. I didn't know what to say, but I ended up taking the envelope with me when I left.

For a large part of my life I have been plagued by the proximity and inevitability of the end. I'm not referring to a predetermined or concrete end, but something much more general and abstract: the end of everything. Something like the spoiling of all the oxygen in the atmosphere, or the putrefaction of the environment, which any minute now might result in the great snuffing out of life. I have always felt that the end was very close to me. It's like an endless *memento mori*. Exhausting.

My relationship with Pablo began when I was exactly eighteen years old. Now I'm forty-three. From the very first day when we went to the movies alone, I waited for the moment he'd tell me he was leaving me. The curious thing about all this is that he actually did leave, but he did it with so many excuses, justifications, promises, and so much twisted guilt that it was one of the few occasions in my life when I couldn't wait until he had finished speaking. In fact, it was as if — just like I had always felt — we had been living a continuous ending, as if our relationship had never even had a beginning.

I'm forty-three years old. Pablo left home on the day of my birthday. He never gave me a single memorable present. Being forty-three years old places me near the end of something. The end of my youth? Perhaps I left that behind a long time ago. Unlike other people when they have their first child, I didn't stop feeling young once Berta was born. Back then I already felt close to the end. I can recall the fear I felt, constantly asking myself what would happen afterwards. When Pablo left me, he blurted out that I had a really strange notion of reality. Now I can laugh about that idea. I don't even think his sentence was put together properly.

In any case, it's at least a little paradoxical that he should be the one to tell me such a thing. I would have liked to have known what his reality would have been like if it weren't for me. But that doesn't matter anymore. Now I'm just worried about Berta and this silly habit she's had for a while. I'm not sure how responsible I am for it. I'm her mother.

Berta is my daughter, and I am twenty kilos overweight. A few months ago, I was already twenty kilos overweight, so it's possible now that I've added a few kilos more. Perhaps the only reason I've decided to write all this down is to become the protagonist of one of those stories of personal triumph in which someone leaves behind all their crippling fears. Writing about how difficult it is to look after yourself consciously, to maintain a healthy diet, to stave off self-destructive impulses and morbid feelings in order to keep things balanced, to find the secret to finally lose weight. I could write a diary — or even better, a blog, like so many people of my generation — explaining all my feelings. If I managed to maintain the diary, I would prove to myself that I'm capable of persevering with things, of creating my own storyline that arrives at a conclusion. That way, I could dissect my problems and look at them from a different perspective, stripping them of dread to the point where I could realise that I was capable of facing up to them. And, by the end, I would be a new woman with a different appearance and a different attitude. That would be my victory.

But I don't think any of that is going to happen. If I have started writing, it's because once again I feel like I'm in one of those moments where I can sense the end of something. The night Pablo told me he was leaving, before he began his endless speech, I already felt that something was about to happen, although I didn't know exactly what. And I had no idea that he had been in love with another person for a long time already.

Shortly after that, I began to scribble down these notes because I felt that something was going to happen to Berta. There were some mornings, as I watched her leave the house, that I became terrified by all the things that might happen to her while she was out of my sight. Soon, I will lose whatever I'm feeling now. We spend our lives losing things. Sometimes I think that all the changes I've experienced across my life haven't amounted to anything; that in fact it's quite the opposite. All they've done is pull apart the world I was born into and that was rightfully mine.

When the artist accompanied my daughter home and burst into our lives, it became the cause of a new conflict. She distrusted him and was irritated by my conciliatory spirit, which I had only adopted to try to follow her teacher's instructions.

'Anyway, the painting is really ugly,' she said.

'That hardly matters. That man is just being friendly. He's worried about you. And I wouldn't be caught up in this mess if you weren't making yourself faint at school. I hope you plan on to telling me what that's all about. I've booked you an appointment with the doctor for a full check-up.'

Berta was furious. Perhaps it fell to me, her mother, to calm her down, but I was unable to do it.

'I don't need to go to the doctor, because there's nothing going on with me, and that man can just leave me alone already,' she exploded. 'I'm sick of running into him all over the place. There's a reason I gave his envelope back to the teacher, you know. Why did you have to bring it home? Why can't you all leave me in peace for once?'

I had no choice but to face up to a situation that had become distressing. I thought that by forty-three I would have arrived at an age where certain abstract anxieties would have gone away, and that the time would have come to defeat the scourge of stark reality. Besides, Pablo's abandoning me had been a warning sign that I was now in the definitive stage of my life. Reality was calling out to me through Berta, telling me to pay attention to the truly important things: I should focus on my career, which I no longer cared for, but which was difficult to change or improve; and I had to look out for my daughter and make sure that as far as possible, both our lives would be the product of pleasant moments, free of anxiety, fear, and yearning. This was one of the conclusions at which I had arrived after many sessions of psychotherapy. And while I was in the middle of this process, the artist appeared, pushing me into an awkward situation. As an adult, I should have been able to thank him for the care he had shown my daughter. That way, I could situate the relationship with that man within the normal, correct parameters of social interaction, in a way that would pose no threat to Berta. The best thing would be to accept the situation as just one more test of maturity.

Perhaps I started writing all this down because I wanted to show myself that I am, in fact, capable of behaving the way one is supposed to behave. By extension, at some point I will also be able to lose those extra twenty kilos, the main thing standing between the world and my true appearance. At times, I'm not the person I seem to be.

In any case, one afternoon I turned up at the studio belonging to the artist who had helped my daughter. The first thing I noticed was the prevailing sense of order and cleanliness.

The place was so clean that it was difficult to believe it could be anyone's workspace. I had seen photos of painters' studios, with half-squeezed tubes of paint, crumpled papers, and scraps of dirty canvas strewn across the floor, amongst the rest of the mess.

The man was exquisitely friendly. At the time I didn't think I'd ever met someone so polite. He spoke softly, so softly that I had to strain to hear him. His corduroy trousers were impeccable, along with his woollen V-neck jumper and the shirt he wore beneath it. At first, he seemed much shorter than I was, but that must have been because of how fragile he looked. I began to doubt whether this man really could have held up my daughter after she fainted, but the expressiveness of his hands dismissed any doubts. His fingers were long and sturdy, and his fingernails perfectly manicured. You could trust him simply from the way he moved his hands.

He asked me how Berta was, and it was hard for me to answer. Any old platitude would have sufficed: a polite expression that would satisfy his interest and keep him at the correct distance that good manners require. However, I hesitated in my answer, which meant that all the conflicts, worries, and insecurities surrounding mine and my daughter's relationship over the past few months rose quite naturally to the surface. He listened while I wove together a tale that was so jumbled, contradictory, and full of doubt that even I was irritated by it. Every time I felt I was falling into an uncomfortable spiral, I tried to cut off the conversation and finish off with the only two words I had come to say: *thank you*. But then I'd start blathering on again, and things got even more complicated. All the while he listened to me, and the greater my despair, the calmer he seemed. It was not lost on me that he was trying to impart some kind of lesson with his silence and his friendliness. I managed to move the centre of attention, to distance it from myself. I thanked him for the painting, and in order to avoid him asking what Berta thought of it, I asked him about his work. I was surprised that there were no paintings on display in his workshop, but it didn't seem polite to ask about it. Despite my rambling, I did manage to find out that he had recently returned to Spain after living abroad for many years, and that he practically lived in hiding in his studio. Although he had very precise manners, he paradoxically gave off a sense of great vitality. I supposed that, as an artist, all of the disquiet of his nature was concentrated in his mind or his soul, or wherever creativity came from. From the few words he spoke, I gleaned that his world was much deeper than I was capable of imagining. He showed me some catalogues from his shows while making observations here and there about his work, pointing out little details that ought not go unnoticed. He had spent almost his entire career in Mexico, where he was a very famous artist.

I was unsettled when I left his studio. To a certain degree, I was ashamed of the way I had behaved with him. But the most powerful feeling was one of admiration. I was in awe of the wider world I had been able to glimpse in just the few words the painter had addressed to me about what he was searching for in his work, and how different artistic expressions connected the essence of the human being. At one point he said that his intention was to unsettle the people who view his work. Of course, he'd managed to unsettle me. I had been so excited by his paintings that I felt privileged and lucky to have stumbled across some kind of treasure that, without a doubt, was going to enrich me.

When you feel good, you don't need to seek out short cuts, or hiding places to shy away from dissatisfaction. But when I got home, I wanted to celebrate this discovery with a nice meal at a bar I knew. It doesn't escape me that eating a huge meal is the exact opposite of what I ought to have done: go home quickly and take out a fancy notebook to write about how art brings balance, drawing us away from the sort of unhappiness that causes us to engage in compulsive and self-sabotaging behaviour. The excitement I felt from our meeting was over the top, and it had dazzled me to the point that I could barely recall what had actually happened. On the face of it, I was unsettled when I left the artist's studio because the existence of a person capable of transmitting such a sense of peace seemed like a great discovery. I'm naturally distrustful of people, which is why encounters like that unsettle me and distance me from the rational explanations I have found for the way of the world. My normal behaviour is at polar opposites from the sort of behaviour that transmits peace, I'm well aware of that. And the problem has grown worse since I've been carrying around twenty or twenty-five extra kilos. I'm not a good-natured person. Once, while watching a Turkish film, I heard a proverb that went something along the lines that the only purpose of human life is to make it better for others. I'd be delighted just to be able to believe that. The fact is, that artist seemed to me like one of those people who is concerned with the wellbeing of others.

On the other hand, my euphoria upon leaving the studio was also due to my conviction that I'd just lived through a defining moment of my life, one of those moments that have a special relevance because they change things that happen afterwards. The sort of moments people refer to when they want to mark the beginning of something important in their own life story. I believed that my conversation with the artist, despite the fact that I had done much more talking than he had, had introduced something new in my life, in my capacity to understand and, at the same time, to describe the way of the world.

I had been drawn closer to Beauty, not just to a hazy sense of peace. I had managed to comprehend the search the painter was immersed in constantly, and which drove him forward, even at his age. Perhaps we're all searching for the same thing, without knowing it. Through his work, that afternoon I became capable of understanding why Beauty is so important: it connects us with something very deep in ourselves, something difficult to explain, like pleasure, a kind of communion with invisible materials that takes us back to our original essence.

In moments like these, it's easy to think that the only thing that can bring meaning to life is the search for Beauty. We are all searching for something beautiful because it calms us, it makes us think that order holds sway and nothing bad could possibly happen. My particular epiphany didn't last long, just until the moment I remembered my daughter's obsession with ugliness and imperfection. Perhaps that's why I needed to go into a bar and eat a huge meal, to face up to the notion that I had a daughter who made herself pass out by interrupting her breathing while waiting for the moment when she could no longer recognise her own reflection in the mirror. Stuffing myself in a bar in the middle of the afternoon was meant to function as a good transition between the world of people searching for the essence of Beauty, and my world, the world where a girl who might have been adorable made sure that everything in her life was ugly.

My excitement lasted long enough for me to call the newspaper and try to convince them to publish an interview with the artist. A long time had passed since I had tried to pitch an article. The last pitches I had sent had been declined, but I tried to convince myself that this time would be different. I even listened to the musicality of the brilliant sentences forming in my mind, which I would write based on the gentle intonation of the artist's responses. The melody of that man's voice would be sustained in stunning prose: my prose.

I figured that the best way to re-establish contact was via the telephone. Isabel was surprised to receive my call. We both said how sorry we were that we hadn't been able to settle on a date for that catch-up we were always promising each other. Right after that, she began listing the names of all the people who'd been fired from the newspaper in the past months.

'Time's running out for the rest of us too; everything is going to shit, and very soon,' she said.

She asked about me — someone had told her that Pablo and I had separated. I found something surreal in that simple affirmation. It felt like a lie. Those words seemed as remote as the ones she used to describe the firing of all those people I knew only by name. I preferred to talk about the artist. I wanted to recoup the energy I had felt after the excitement of my visit to the studio. When I began to list the reasons I thought it would be interesting to publish an interview in the newspaper, it felt, after a while, like someone who wasn't me was speaking in a way that I might have spoken, a long time ago. Journalism was no good for me, or maybe I was no good for journalism. Perhaps I was unlucky, and I'd entered the profession when the death-rattles the editor-in-chief had just described to me had already begun to be heard. But having already taken the step of getting back in touch, I kept on listing my reasons.

Isabel wasn't sure that now was the right moment to dedicate so much space to the artist. Throughout our conversation, she demonstrated that she was quite familiar with his trajectory, and she was surprised that Vicente Rojo was in our city. She'd heard that he had only just left Mexico. She asked me if he was preparing a new show, because that would be the perfect reason to include him in the paper. If we didn't have a convincing reason, something tied to the frenetic nature of the news cycle, it would be hard for her to secure space in the newspaper's pages. I told her that the people at Berta's school had said that he would be giving classes there. Isabel went quiet for a moment, but in the end, she encouraged me to interview him, to find out what he was doing here, and to get to the bottom of the business of the art classes at the school. Before hanging up, she said I should check my diary and come by the newsroom one day to see my old colleagues. I would never be able to go back there. That was a world I had left behind long ago, but I was determined to write a great interview with the artist, Vicente Rojo.

I tried to share with Berta the epiphany I'd had while visiting the artist's studio, but she still didn't want to hear about it.

'And I'd appreciate it,' she said, 'if you wouldn't leave the painting where I might see it. Every time I look at it, even when it's by accident, it looks worse and worse to me.' I persisted until she said something like how it came as no surprise that all this was happening to her, because it was just another stop on her journey along the highway of horror. Without waiting for me to respond, she added that, on the other hand, she would be very thankful if I let her have a pet.

'So it feels like I have company,' she said. Because I still hadn't reacted to her words, she took the opportunity to reproach me: 'But it has to be a really repulsive pet, really ugly and horrible, otherwise it won't be a good match for me.' When at last I spoke, I told her she couldn't have a pet while she persisted with this attitude and with living so chaotically. She looked me straight in the eyes with an ironic smile that I had never seen before. I held her gaze in silence, until she was the one to look away, returning to the piece of paper she had been doodling on while I had been trying to hold a conversation with her.

I thought she'd lost interest in drawing some time ago, but I realised that she had returned to the habit of drawing tiny, irregular circles, each one squeezed next to the other. They looked like minuscule pebbles, forming a shapeless, pimply mass that seemed to expand across the page like a sponge, or milk spots on the skin.

I wasn't ready to give in to her desire to change the topic of conversation. I told her that the newspaper had asked me to interview the artist, because he was very famous in Mexico. She kept on with the circles, tracing over them without looking at me, as if she hadn't heard me at all. She never gave me the opportunity to tell her about the importance of Beauty in discovering an essential part of one's existence. She had asked me for a pet, the ugliest I could find, and I begged her to tell me what kind of animal she wanted. I also asked her not to adopt an animal that was sick, wounded, or deformed. By the way she looked at me, I knew I had stumbled across her plans. Then she made me feel guilty.

'Okay, nothing sick, nothing deformed, healthy animals only. Are fat animals healthy? What about skinny ones?'

The artist asked me to come to his studio for the interview. He said it was the place where he felt safest, that he almost never left his house and that when he did, the studio was where he went. I was amazed once again by how clean and orderly the place was. We sat at the same table as the first time I'd visited, in the corner, on the old wicker chairs that had been restored. On the wall opposite the table, a wooden structure, similar to a shelf, housed canvasses that had been arranged neatly in a row, as if they were books. I distracted myself by imagining the paintings on the canvases.

He had laid out a teapot on the table, along with two cups and a packet of biscuits. He continued to demonstrate the same impeccable manners as last time, but it was clear that he felt uncomfortable. He'd let me know over the phone that he was happy to chat with me for a while, but doubted that anything he had to say would be of any use for the interview. As soon as he had welcomed me into the studio for the second time, he repeated his objections. When I left the tape recorder on the table, I noticed his displeasure. To reassure him, I reminded him that the editor of the culture section had seemed very interested in the possibility of publishing an interview with him. It was meant as a compliment, but it just made him even more uncomfortable.

'You never told me you were a journalist.'

'Actually, I haven't written for the newspaper in a long time, but after our conversation the other day I got interested in interviewing you and publishing it.'

'I don't know who would be interested in anything I have to say. I'm just a very old man who no longer understands the world. I don't even know what the world is anymore. Even if I did know, I wouldn't know how to express it. Every time I've been interviewed, I've always regretted it afterwards. I'm frustrated by my inability to explain what I think.'

'You have lots of interesting things to say. And it's a real pleasure to listen while you speak. I've been looking online and I have to admit I've been surprised by how much information there is about you. I'm ashamed of my ignorance.'

'What do you mean?'

'I mean I'm ashamed to say that until now I was completely unaware of your work. You're very important. You work is very well-known.'

He looked down and raised his hand slightly, as if he wished to silence me, but didn't quite dare. He smiled.

'There are still a few people interested in my work, yes. And believe me, I've worked a lot, always. Working for culture is working for life.'

'I've seen a lot of your work online: graphic design, sculpture ... And of course, the legendary cover of *One Hundred Years of Solitude*.'

'Where did you say you saw all of this? What catalogue was it?'

'I saw it online. On the internet.'

Not only had Vicente Rojo never heard of the internet, he also tried to convince me that no such thing existed. I tried to explain it to him, and told him about the vast network of computers where it was possible to gain access to any type of information you wanted, and all you had to do was type in a few words, like, for example, 'Vicente Rojo'. He laughed in my face. He even went so far as to say that a person with even a shred of intelligence wouldn't waste their time on absurd machines or with extravagant theories about knowledge and culture.

'There's only one way to learn. It's been the same for thousands of years, and it's going to stay the same, believe me. But it means less and less every day. Everyone distracts themselves with lies and illusions. Like many others, I have dedicated my existence to the struggle in which the essential aims to take ground from the banal, which, through its vulgar commercialisation, ushers in all manner of things that are secondary, irrelevant, quick, and easy.'

He spoke with such conviction that he managed to make me

feel absurd for trying to make him understand how useful the internet and other innovative technologies can be.

'And what's the point of all these computers?' he asked. When I didn't respond, he continued. 'To keep on degrading us, that's all. Sometimes I think they'll get what they want: that we'll stop thinking, that we'll stop wanting to see visions of the world different from theirs. Nowadays, the only way people want to look at reality is the way they taught us.'

This last comment made me think of the perception experiments my daughter was interested in.

So, Vicente Rojo and Berta appeared to be joined by some invisible thread, two accomplices who had been completely unaware of each other, despite the fact that they were mired in the same search. This was exactly why they had found each other. I could only watch on from a distance and try to understand whatever it was that moved them. That's why I had decided to write.

The artist continued talking about how the powerful tried to impose their way of understanding reality, in which everything in the world seemed to have an assigned value that was accepted willingly.

'It's very important to maintain a healthy distance with respect to all the noise and ruckus to be able to see anything. One of the most transcendental experiences of my life was a time when, as a young man, I was taken to the peak of a mountain in Mexico. From there I could see the valley. Everything was very small. The landscape was reduced to tiny stains of colour, and in those little smudges, the essence of the world was distilled. I suppose that's why I dedicated myself to painting, because I wanted to replicate those landscapes, the colour of the material that defines us. That's when I understood the importance of maintaining the proper distance from everything, and that's perhaps the thought that has helped me the most in my life.'

He sat in silence, as if weighing the meaning of everything he had just said, or as if his thoughts had taken him back to the peak of that mountain where he had experienced his revelation. I didn't want to interrupt him, and besides, I was lost in my own thoughts.

My daughter was already ahead of me. At only fifteen, she was deep in a search that compelled her, at the very least, towards the sort of reflection that would undoubtedly lead to something fruitful. Maybe it wouldn't be an epiphany like Vicente Rojo's on that mountain in Mexico, but surely it would help her arrive at some conclusion that would help her to resist. Even at my age, I have none of these transformative experiences to relate, which means I also have no theories or explanations that would help me understand existence or to face up to reality, nothing that could even help me with the constant pummelling of frustration. My old classmates from university and colleagues from my first jobs were able to come up with their own theories. Some wrote books about them: books about social groups, literary trends, the future of human relations and communication ... I'm not exaggerating when I say that it's difficult for me to think for myself. My way of functioning has more to do with finding a reference or authority that gives credit to an idea I'm trying to manifest. Problems arise when I can't find anyone to articulate the formless idea that's tormenting me. There are so many theories and so many explanations that I find it hard to see myself in any of them, to feel that, at last, I have found an explanation of the world from which I can build a safe and secure life. When I lived with Pablo, everything was easier, because I just followed in his footsteps. Our life was made up of the routines he had established, and he managed to convince me they worked for me too. Pablo was the reference point I needed because, unlike me, he seemed sure of what steps to take. In any case, I'm not going to talk about him, because he has absolutely nothing to do with what's going on here, because this is about trying to give shape to an ethical model. That might sound pompous, but that's what I was looking for: a way to define the rules that ordered Vicente Rojo's life. How to interact with one's surroundings, with nature, with animals, with other human beings. How to improve the lives of others so that your own isn't so frustrating. How to find meaning in the events that come together to form a life. In the end, it was comforting to listen to the artist because he had his own story about the creation and development of the world. Building from everything he had experienced, he had articulated his own personal discourse: words upon which he had built his life, and which protected him. And he'd managed to do all that without Google or the internet.

The interview was a failure. I couldn't shake the sensation that the artist looked down on me because I had no thoughts of my own. He was looking for a dialectic, an interlocutor with whom he might exchange opinions, and I wasn't up to it. I just swallowed and blinked when it looked like he wanted to ask me something, held my breath every time he couldn't recall the name of an artist or a musician or a philosopher and looked at me for help. I sighed with relief when eventually he came up with the name he was looking for.

All in all, what was supposed to be my triumphant return to the newspaper was just a failed and frustrating interview. However, for some nagging reason that I won't stop to analyse here, I wasn't ready to give up. I'd had the great fortune of Vicente Rojo stumbling into my boring little life, and I had to make the most of it. What's more, he'd spent the whole afternoon saying interesting things, so I felt obliged to stick with it and learn something from him. Once, somebody asked me why I liked journalism. After thinking about it for a long time, all I could think to say was that it was a job where you were constantly learning new things. When I think of that answer now, I can't help giving a wry smile, but that afternoon, when I interviewed Vicente Rojo, I still believed something similar, and I was absolutely prepared to make the effort to learn whatever it was that the artist was trying to explain to me, and which, without a doubt, would enrich my life. With a little luck, and by taking on some of his life lessons as my own, perhaps I could even lose a few kilos. He didn't seem like the sort of person who needed to deal with anxiety by regularly gorging himself; in fact, it seemed like he had accepted his fragility and knew how to behave in harmony with his own nature.

This didn't seem so easy once I got home and tried to transcribe the interview. The conversation was a total disaster, and not because (as he had said at the start of the interview) he couldn't put his thoughts into words, but because of my absurd questions. I had to accept that it would be impossible for me to get a profile or a worthwhile article out of the material. But I needed to know more about the artist, about his desire to work in culture, which for him meant 'working for life'. I wanted to learn more about the independence and knowledge he had obtained, thanks to the healthy distance he maintained from the noise, shadows, and figures that make up reality. It was precisely because of this famous distance and perspective that he had been able to paint so well. I wanted to learn more from Vicente Rojo because I thought I had found the moral and intellectual authority that I had been lacking for so long. That was the deficiency that explained the brainlessness and mediocrity I had been living in.

That's when I had a new vision. Everything that had been going wrong for me would be fixed if I wrote an essay about Vicente Rojo's thinking. I had seen online that other people had written about his paintings, his sculptures, and his work in graphic design, but that didn't discourage me, because it was unlikely that anyone had delved as deep into the artist's thoughts as I would. And if I took Vicente Rojo at his word, and decided to believe that the internet doesn't exist, then how could any such study possibly be out there? That's how I had come to understand the artist's unwillingness to believe in the world-wide web: the only things that exist are those that one incorporates into one's own existence and that adapt into a tool for the interpretation of one's moment in time and space. I wouldn't be unsettled by what others had said, because what truly mattered was what *I* was going to learn from the artist and the way in which all these elements would come together to achieve balance.

While I was trying to transcribe that terrible first interview, Berta sidled up to the table where I was working. She didn't even try to hide her annoyance when she saw I was working on something related to Vicente Rojo.

'Why did you interview him? He's so annoying. Did you tell him to leave me alone? That's all I asked you to do. And to give him back the painting.'

'He's a very important artist, Berta. I don't know why you've got yourself so worked up about him. As far as I can tell, he was the only one who bothered to help you, and then he gave you a painting. You don't know how lucky you are. And if you showed just a tiny amount of interest in what he does, I think you'd like it. You're fifteen years old, it's time you started paying attention to culture, art, literature ...'

She interrupted me.

'An important artist? Why have they banned him from giving classes at school? The art teacher didn't allow it. He's a weirdo. Mario, Lucas, and I always see him around the school, snooping. I'm almost afraid of him, and Lucas says that one day he saw him going through the rubbish. I bet he's just a bum who's managed to sweet-talk you.'

At that moment I was aware, as I am now, that my daughter was provoking me, and that for some time she had been trying to start a fight between us. Although it would be a total cliché, it's possible she blamed me for the fact that her father had abandoned us. I usually tried to ignore her provocations, but that afternoon she managed to get under my skin.

'You have no idea what you're talking about. It's absolutely true that we're lucky to have met this man. Why are you saying all this? And what's this little expression, that he "sweet-talked" me? It's nasty and offensive. Where did you learn that?'

'Dad says it,' she said quickly, as if she wished to be rid of the words and transfer them to me. It had already happened — she would no longer be the sole recipient of her father's comments — so she changed the subject, almost as if she was trying to patch things up. 'Anyway, I just wanted to tell you that I've decided which pet I want. It's called a hermit ibis, it's a type of bird.'

The conversation up to this point had unsettled and irritated me. I didn't want to talk to her about her father, and I'd thought he and I had an agreement that neither of us would talk badly about the other in front of Berta. I had never heard of the animal she was talking about, but when she mentioned it was a bird,

I knew straight away that she was trying to provoke me again, even though we both knew it would be best if we avoided another fight. I said nothing. That glint of irony and disdain flickered in her eyes again. She seemed much older than she was, and in her smile, I could detect a hint of malice. She left me alone again, and I kept on with my transcribing.

On the shelves and tables and furniture in the house that Berta and I share, it's quite common to find little papers of all kinds, on which Berta has drawn tiny circles. I thought of those scribblings while I read one of the articles about painting that I was thinking of using as a source for my essay on Vicente Rojo. I thought of the bubbling lava that my daughter would draw while I read a fragment of something written by Mark Rothko, where he says he arrived at abstract painting because artists like him were fleeing the idea of representation. Artists search for themselves; they no longer seek ideal forms, representations of beauty, death, or pain. My daughter searches for herself in those little circles she draws incessantly. The amorphous mass of them reveals something to her, although I doubt even she knows what it is. It's the same way that Vicente Rojo seeks meaning in geometric forms, in squares, pyramids, or friezes.

One night I dreamt that an ibis was stalking down the hallway of our apartment. It was holding a wad of papers in its long beak, all of them covered in Berta's little circles. The floor, the furniture, every single surface in the house was covered with papers. It was hard to tell if the ibis was trying to clean up all the papers in its beak, or if it was trying to scatter them all over the place. The bird walked nervously from one end of the apartment to the other, kicking up papers from the floor as it did so. I'd never seen the particular species of bird that Berta wanted for a pet, but, of course, I had looked it up online. The animal toiling away among the papers in my hallway was larger than that species tends to be, which is about seventy-five centimetres tall. The ibis in my dream was nearly as tall as a person. It turned my stomach to see its bald, featherless head, the same pinkish colour as a newborn baby. The beak was very long and of the same colour, and stood out against the filthy grey of the papers it held. The bald pink head was framed by a crown of long black feathers that led down to the bird's neck, also covered in black feathers, but shorter ones, which gave off little iridescent reflections of metallic green.

I tried to follow the bird's frenetic movements, but it was impossible. The ibis could never quite take hold of any of the papers that flew up around it. It was impossible to tell if they were covered in tiny little circles, as I had originally thought, or if they were covered with words: the questions and answers I needed for my interview with Vicente Rojo. In fact, the whole scene was taking place with some soft background music, and it was also impossible to tell if it was the artist's melodious voice on my tape recorder, or the desperate croaking of the bird, exhausted by its unmanageable task.

At some point in the dream, I realised that the bird had become my daughter, without changing shape: the same shaved head, the same dark, messy plumage, which could be one of the huge jumpers she hides herself in. My daughter, transformed into a horrible bird in my hallway, wandering around my apartment, which was slowly filling up with dirty, indecipherable papers, and there was nothing I could do to help her.

That nightmare upset me, and I returned to it again and again over the following days, to the extent that I even recounted it to Vicente Rojo the next time we met. Of course, I left out the part where his singsong voice might have formed part of the soundtrack. We began by discussing the constant anxiety one feels during one's adolescent years. As you might expect, he spoke not of sensations he felt some seventy years ago, but as if he was recalling events that had just taken place. That's how vivid his memories were. The fear he felt at having to go to school — which for him was the place where his strongest hand, his left, was always being tied back — was mixed with the memory of his excitement at discovering the light in Mexico in the moment he considers his second birth. He told me that just by looking at Berta he could tell she was an intelligent girl, so intelligent that she would undoubtedly suffer for the rest of her life. As her mother, I told him, I hoped she would eventually learn to use her intelligence precisely to *avoid* suffering for her whole life. My comment seemed to annoy him. I continued to be an interlocutor unworthy of his thoughts and experiences.

'Lucidity and intelligence are a privilege. Disdaining it is an insult to the species, to the essence of human nature. We must take responsibility for what we have received in life. Sometimes it's not much, but because of the fact of having been born and living where we do, we are obliged to take responsibility and act accordingly, because we too are an essential part of the whole. If I see a young woman faint while she's staring closely at one of my paintings, I am obliged to help her and take an interest in her, to make sure that she is OK and that nothing bad has happened. As long as it's within reach. You know what? Everything I am, everything that defines me, is right here, in my hands. I am whatever they are capable of doing. I discovered this at a very young age, and ever since I've done nothing but test them out, try to listen to them, to see how they manifest, what they need, how they wish to communicate with the world.'

But after he had raised his hands to show them to me, he lay them back in his lap. In the growing silence, I limited myself to looking at my notebook, and then we continued talking about my daughter and her obsession with drawing little circles on whatever piece of paper was put in front of her. He told me I had no right to criticise her, much less ban her from it, because she was looking for a way to communicate something, even if she was the only recipient of this coded message. He said that reproaching her for her obsession with drawing little circles would be like tying back her strong hand.

'Creating areas of shadow and doubt is what gives meaning to art.' This is one of the sentences I wrote down in the notebook I clung to whenever he spoke. Back then I didn't believe, and I still don't believe now, that Berta has a special inclination or an exceptional talent when it comes to artistic endeavours. But it was clear that she was immersed in a very determined search. The little circles, at first glance, revealed Berta's need to fill the void. From within the void it's difficult to find a possible location from which one might try to understand things. That's why it's easier to surround oneself with objects, with a kind of lava that fills the mind and even the eyes: once you're in the middle of this lava, all you need to worry about is breathing and holding on.

I also spoke to Vicente Rojo about my daughter's other obsession, the pet. That's when I told him about my dream where the ibis scattered papers all through my house. I also told him how at the end of the dream, I was upset to see that the bird was actually my daughter. I don't know if he was trying to console me, but he told me that we should never be afraid of what our brain sees or imagines, because it's the only way to gain access to the higher functions of our existence. Beyond the impact of seeing Berta transformed into a bird, something which could obviously never occur, I should ask myself what the image meant and why it scared me so much.

I had begun to be exasperated by the fact that my daughter insisted on asking for an ibis, and that she was refusing to acknowledge that it would be impossible to have one as a pet. It was an endangered species that only lived in Morocco and Syria — Syria, where everything at the time seemed in danger of extinction because of the brutal war. Why was my daughter insisting on one of those birds? She had led us into an absurd situation, with no solution, and it seemed like she was unwilling to get us out of it.

In the beginning I didn't pay much attention to her request, because it was obvious we couldn't have a bird like that at home. But the longer she insisted, the more the bird began to take shape until it became a true presence. Sometimes I wasn't sure if she was using the bird to demand some kind of special attention I wasn't giving her, and at other times I had the feeling we spoke about the bird as if it were an incarnation of her father, and she wanted it to take up the space he had willingly abandoned. The conversations about that ugly bird became so absurd that it should have come as no surprise that I started dreaming that it had become a part of our daily lives, running up and down the hall.

The artist listened to me attentively while I told him about the problem of the pet. I thought he'd mention Berta's intelligence and its consequences once again. However, after a silence that made me think I'd gone on too long with my complaints and explanations, he returned to the topic of his childhood.

'When I was barely seven years old, I witnessed something painful. I lived in the city with my family, and we had suffered greatly from the war. I watched as removalists took the piano my sisters used to play out of our apartment, via the window on the fifth floor. My sisters loved the piano, and it was probably the last item of value my family had to sell. I watched the spectacle of the piano movers and it caused me great pain and anxiety.'

Another phrase I jotted down in my notebook: 'Over seventy years later, the same kid, his hands full of papers and coloured pencils, thinks that across his whole life, his greatest desire, the thing that has kept him awake at night, has been the desire to get that piano back.' As if to link that sentence with a concrete image, I remember I looked around for a pencil like the one he had described, first in his hands and then somewhere in the studio, but I couldn't see a single one. That's why I'm not sure if what surprised me most was the vivid image of that boy long ago, or the fact that the man who had been the boy had no pencil in his hand at that exact moment.

Of course, I understood what Vicente Rojo wanted me to understand through his story about the piano. Throughout his whole life, the artist he became never stopped hunting, reading, and learning as he searched for an answer that would ease the anxiety of the boy he had been, who had never been able to understand why the piano was taken away. But the pain was still there, so many years later. My daughter had begun her own quest to understand her anxiety, but she had drawn me into it too, which is why she demanded I provide her with a reason why we couldn't have a huge, disgusting bird in our apartment. It's not the same as having a piano at all. The scene narrated by Vicente Rojo was terrible, which is why he had had to work so hard his whole life to temper it, at the very least, even if he could never fully understand it. On the other hand, what Berta wanted was for me to convince her that a more beautiful life existed, one where it wouldn't matter that she couldn't have a huge, ugly bird at home. She wanted me to disagree with her and tell her that it wasn't true that she would only ever have the ugly things in life. I could intuit the parallels laid out by the artist, but that doesn't mean I was able to extract anything useful to confront my daughter and make her understand it was impossible to have an ibis at home. It's a truly disgusting bird.

By the artist's reckoning, abjection can be just as attractive and enriching as Beauty. In the end, they're just two sides of the same coin: the presence and absence of beauty. This made Vicente Rojo think of a painter he had met in France, a Dutch artist named Bram van Velde. He told me that all van Velde wished to express in his painting was misery, disquiet, anxiety, and the constant suffering of someone doomed to pursue the unattainable. Bram van Velde himself said that his painting sought out ugliness and madness. I wrote his name down so I could google his paintings later, and when I eventually saw them, I found them truly beautiful. I was struck by the fact that while Vicente Rojo's paintings were all about balance, in van Velde's work there was a kind of frenzied energy, figures that seem to want to spring from the canvas, forms and colours that seem to be at war with each other but which the painter has managed to capture at precisely the moment they achieve equilibrium. I dared to conclude that although the way abstraction worked was different for both painters, in the end they weren't so far apart: they had both found different forms of balance.

When I announced to Vicente Rojo that I was planning to write an essay on his thinking as well as the interview, he became uncomfortable and said he was against it. He said he didn't want to put himself on a pedestal as some sort of model or example for anyone else, because he had never been able to stand the cult of personality. He told me an anecdote that he'd heard from Miguel Prieto, whom he considered to be one of his masters. When Prieto was a boy, he had to walk several kilometres a day to get to school in Almodóvar del Campo. Many years later, he found out that every day his father would follow him along for some of the way, watching on without him knowing, so that he could grow in self-confidence. According to Vicente Rojo, Prieto became emotional whenever he was in Mexico, so far from the town of his childhood, and remembered all the trouble his father went to, following him and protecting him without being seen. From this lesson from his teacher, Vicente Rojo had learnt such fundamental things as discretion, subtlety, simplicity, and warmth.

Our conversation that afternoon dragged on through anecdotes that might have been parables, and through phrases apparently destined to become aphorisms or mantras. I wrote one of them down in my notebook: 'I welcome all imperfections, and I'm thankful for surprises. The errors we make, just like accidents, can turn out to be stimulating. I have no reason to hide my faults; in fact, I try to get something useful out of them.' He was referring to his method of working, which made me doubt the degree to which we were actually talking about the same thing. I can understand that ugliness, mistakes, the abject, and a lack of balance represent true challenges for an artist aspiring to beauty or at least emotion, but I was referring to the fascination Berta had for all things ugly. Strictly speaking, it wasn't even a real fascination, because she considered ugliness as a part of her reality, but not without a certain degree of resignation and resentment. What I wanted to know is whether, deep down, she would like to be on the other side, before mistakes or accidents come into the frame, when she could still master balance and serenity. Sometimes I'm convinced she's asking me for some kind of magic spell that would place her forever on that side. And I can't do it.

In any case, my daughter's attraction for the darker, dirtier side of existence is nothing new when it comes to people, and especially not for teenagers. I suppose that, in my search for answers, I could look into the most primal customs and expressions (whether private or collective) of human beings, back when we began to become aware of our condition. Further down the line I could look into black magic, superstitions, witches, spells, and all the rest of it.

Now, in my mind, I confuse what I thought during the interview with what the artist said, the notes I took and what I thought upon reflection afterwards. I was sure that in there somewhere I would find a nice paragraph for my essay on the attraction human beings feel for things we don't like, and how that pushes us to explore Nature and everything it is capable of, the diverse manifestations of how far life can push us. In the end, we are the fruit of chance, of a few lucky combinations of chemical and matter. It's quite normal that we would want to speculate about our potential as human beings, because by knowing what we could become, what might happen to us, with our bodies and our environment, the people who surround us, the objects we possess and that we like to observe, then we would learn a tiny bit more about ourselves. That's why horror excites us. Just as we seek out experiences of beauty, when we are presented with its absence, our spirit also experiences a union with the true essence, the energy we belong to. Which is to say, we can be pure energy without form or meaning, a bubbling magma capable of anything or nothing; or, on the other hand, we can accept beauty and allow it to give us form, balance, and meaning. Some people call this essence God, or Nature, or simply light, but when we are immersed in it, we are beyond the physical or sensorial limits of our brains. Vicente Rojo said that the clearest example of this communion, which could be pleasurable or painful, is the emotion we feel when listening to music or observing a masterpiece.

All of these ideas were jumbled and poorly developed in my notes. But they were going to help me nail down Vicente Rojo's aesthetic, ethical, and philosophical models, first in the interview, and later in the essay. It would be a kind of necessary moral guide in times of turmoil. I was thinking of drawing up a document that would help the reader to stride purposefully through all the challenges posed during a lifetime, especially in moments like the one I was currently experiencing. To begin with, I had decided to stop feeling like I was on the edge of the abyss, at the end of everything, full of fear that a black hole was about to swallow me and everything I held dear. The artist had managed to expand the boundaries of my existence, boundaries I had always considered to be so limiting, so close and threatening.

In my notes from those interviews I highlighted a few important words, and two stood out especially: *imagination* and *hope*. Vicente Rojo made me see that imagination isn't only important for artists, but for everyone in their daily lives. Existence in itself can be reduced to just a few things, which is why it's so important to endow them with meaning that gives us pleasure or happiness. What we seek is emotion, in a word. None of this is possible without imagination, which is nourished by what we already know, what we learn every day from our most immediate reality, but also through the feelings inspired by art, literature, music, and other sensations that are difficult to name. The artist's other word, *hope*, makes me despair. I think it's heavily linked with imagination. To have hope, it is essential to be able to imagine what we hope for. That's where I was stuck. However, the essay I wanted to write would be rigorous, so I had to stay on the margins. I was struggling to keep the chaos of my life out of the story I was trying to tell. I had to distil the artist's way of thinking, his exemplary life, his model of living, which was so different from what my life with Pablo had been, and what my life without him had started to become. My only aim was to write a narrative, with a beginning and an end, that could endow existence with meaning, to create a life that was worthy. 'To change the world, you need imagination and good timing,' said Vicente Rojo.

Listening to him talk comforted me because of the enveloping musicality of his voice, and the serenity that radiated from the images he conjured. I read, or heard somewhere, that there's a hormone that causes a gland in the brain to release a substance that induces pleasure in certain moments. It happens during pregnancy too, I think. I'm convinced my brain was secreting a substance similar to that while I listened to him talk, and while I enjoyed that moment of happiness, I felt I would be able to confront Berta and tell her that I no longer cared that she wanted to surround herself with ugly things, because I knew that was good, that that way she'd learn about beautiful things too. In any case, we were never going to be able to have an ibis in the apartment, because it was impossible. But there was nothing to stop her investigating the nature of her desires and the feelings associated with the image of the bird.

Obviously, when I had Berta right in front of me, at home, I was unable to say any of the things I had thought about and jotted down while I was at the artist's studio. She continued to torture me with questions about the bird, asking me if I'd done anything to see if we could have an ibis at home. Since I had begun my interview and essay project, every time I sat down at the desk in the study, which used to be occupied by Pablo, I had an argument with my daughter. And it always went the same way. In the beginning, I refused to answer questions about the bird, until her language became so rude that I realised we were no longer talking about the ibis. The conversation I'm recalling now didn't follow this formula. Berta said that she had looked into it and found out that a few years ago, the ibis had been successfully reintroduced into some mountainous areas and national parks in Cádiz. So, I was wrong when I told her that the bird only lived in Morocco and Syria.

'To begin with,' she explained, 'the hermit ibis is too big to be referred to simply as a bird. You use the word bird for the tiny little varieties. Secondly, the reintroduction of the species after an absence of five centuries is underway, and it has been successful in Cádiz.'

'I see you've been talking about the bird with your father. Maybe he's been able to convince you that it's impossible to have an ibis as a pet in the house?'

'They have them in Cádiz.'

I asked Berta if she wanted to move to Cádiz.

'Or wherever,' she said.

The image of a seven-year-old boy watching his sister's piano being taken out of the house through the window returned to me, the piano whose music had filled so many childhood afternoons.

'But you can't have an ibis as a pet in Cádiz either.'

Berta let out a huff of impatience, then turned around and left me to my papers.

I had become obsessed with writing the essay and had let go of the idea of publishing the interview with Vicente. Isabel had called again to ask me about it and to see if I'd found out anything more about what had brought the artist to our city. One of her bosses had become interested and had committed to a big spread covering the artist's work. She also asked me if, in the end, Vicente Rojo would be giving classes at the high school. 'Your daughter is so lucky, what an experience,' she said. If that was the case, they'd even send a photographer, and they'd ask me to include some testimonials from the sessions. I didn't have the courage to tell her that, for some strange reason that I couldn't understand, Berta hated Vicente Rojo. I didn't tell her, either, that Berta's art teacher wasn't letting him give any classes.

While my conversation with Isabel was becoming confused, in my mind the essay I was going to write was perfectly structured. I could hear the melody of the prose, with the same intonation as Vicente Rojo's voice when he spoke. I told her I had several hours of conversation recorded, but that I didn't think I'd got to the heart of his personality yet.

'Don't go over the top with your research,' she said. 'All you need to do is write a profile. Go through his background and his work, but most of all, I think it'd be interesting to reflect on the relationship between the artist and the students: if they're interested in his work, if they cared about his experiences in exile, you know, something about what the younger generations think of illustrious figures who are already the last link to another time, another world.'

After hearing all of this, I still wasn't able to reveal the fact that my daughter had already told me that there would be no classes. We agreed that I would call Isabel back soon, because the deadline was looming, and no other newspaper had published a story about Vicente Rojo yet. If we were the first to break the story, we would be able to say that *our newspaper* was still the most avant-garde, the most advanced, and the most dedicated to the promotion of culture. Vicente Rojo hadn't mentioned that any other journalists had approached him, or that any other newspapers were interested in covering his stay in our city. I was certain there was no one else writing about him. But it's true that when I saw the number of articles, monographs, and catalogues related to his work online, I felt discouraged and thought I'd never be able to write anything interesting, nothing that added to what had already been said. But I was clinging to the artist, because I wanted to turn him into something much more important than a famous painter: he was going to be a moral beacon, as well as an aesthetic benchmark. At that moment in my life, the most important thing was writing about the artist. From the very beginning, he had appeared as the perfect foil for my daughter. Now that I think about it, perhaps I thought that by understanding Vicente Rojo, I would also be able to understand my daughter.

Isabel's haste for me to send her the article or the interview (or whatever it was) as soon as possible, and her interest in the viewpoints of the students taking the art classes, gave me enough encouragement to make another appointment with Vicente Rojo. He invited me to meet once more in his impeccable studio. On that afternoon, he was holding a pencil in his right hand. Although I had arrived at the agreed-upon time, I had the feeling that perhaps I had interrupted him, but there were no notebooks or any other materials on his work table that he could have been using to sketch. I couldn't help thinking about the bits of paper covered in circles that Berta leaves all over the house.

I told him how my editor at the newspaper was asking for me to turn in the interview (or the report, or whatever it would be), and asked him why there were some aspects of his life that we had barely covered. He was surprised that I still didn't have enough material for the article, given how long our meetings had been. I had no choice but to tell him that in our previous interviews, we'd spent more time talking about me and Berta than him.

'Well then, write about yourself. It would definitely be more interesting.'

I couldn't tell if it was modesty that led him to speak to me in this way, or if he was being ironic because he was annoyed.

'There's nothing interesting about my life, you can be sure of that. But at the newspaper, they think it would be very interesting to report on your visit and to follow along during your classes with the students.'

That afternoon the artist was more visibly affected than in previous visits. It was difficult to pick up on it, because he spoke with the same warmth, and his movements and gestures showed the same sense of balance that had fascinated me last time. But I heard him clear his throat for the first time. And after he cleared his throat, he let out a very subtle sigh. That's how he confirmed what Berta had already told me: he wouldn't be giving any classes at the school. It was clear he was annoyed, so if I truly wanted to extend the conversation, I had no choice but to take the reins myself.

'My daughter told me there still isn't a fixed date for the start of painting classes, but even so, I'd like to start writing the report.'

'It makes me sad to see the people entrusted with your children's education. Imagining their future is terrible. They're supposed to be our great hope, don't you think?' He paused, but I knew not to interrupt. 'Don't think that now I'll fall into the role of the bitter old man who pines for his youth and thinks that no other generation could possibly be as great as his own. I honestly hope that no other generation has to go through what mine did. But it's truly disheartening to see what's going on now. Those people who call themselves teachers aren't interested in my classes, or anything I could teach the students. Here, nobody knows who I am. And that doesn't surprise me at all. These kids are the product of previous generations who spent too long navel-gazing, denying the existence of anything happening outside their own field of vision. But I don't blame them. Maybe it wasn't even that important.'

'I could speak with the school's principal, or the director of studies? It would be a shame for the kids to miss out on the privilege of taking classes with you. I could write about all this in the article, then they'd have to let you teach the classes, right?'

For a few seconds he looked me in the eyes silently. He seemed startled and defeated in equal parts. The calm and balance that had made such an impression on me in our first meetings had disappeared from his gaze. He was begging for help. But I wasn't the person to give him the care he needed. His gaze managed to unsettle me just as much as Berta's. I never seemed to be up to what he asked of me.

After a few moments, he smiled.

'My dear, you have understood very little of all this, barely a thing. It would be crazy to denounce all of this in the newspaper. What would be the point? It could only bring us problems. And it makes me ask myself, why do you want to write about me? I've already told you that the only thing that matters to me is my work. If you like, you can write about that; I can lend you one of my catalogues. Your daughter's school has also informed me that they will be returning the painting I gave them. They say they have no room for such a large work. Excuses. Then it occurred to me that I could give the painting to you, and you could write about it.'

His voice still had the same musicality, but he couldn't hide the fact that he was agitated. He gripped his pencil tightly, as if it were a weapon, or as if the object itself could confer him with a sense of authority that demanded respect. I'm not sure why he thought of giving the painting to me, or if he was truly expecting an answer to the question of why I wanted to write about him. I could have told him that I was at a point in my life where I was feeling truly disoriented, that I was afraid of the proximity of the end of something I couldn't identify, that I didn't know where to look to find meaning, that I rejected the way I looked, my present, everything I had done with my life in these forty-three years, that whatever might happen from here was a great unknown that I was too scared to think about, that I didn't feel strong enough to plan anything, that the only identifiable desire I had (and which I had often) was to get the hell out of here, to move anywhere but here, to Mexico like him, or to Cádiz, with Berta and the ibises, or even better, to go somewhere by myself to try to escape this looming ending that had pursued me my whole life. But I couldn't tell him any of this, because at that moment I was obliged to write something about Vicente Rojo, the artist and intellectual, master of equilibrium, who would serve as a guide to me and other people equally as desperate.

Why didn't I realise that the best thing I could do right then would be to get the hell out of his studio? Not only did I fail to do that, I tried to ease things by leading the conversation in another direction.

'My editor also thought it would be interesting if you spoke about your experience of exile.'

'My experience of exile? Do you know who Max Aub is? Have you read *The Blind Chicken*? That's the best book about exile.'

I had read some Max Aub; I think it was a novel about the concentration camps, and all I could recall is that I thought he had a funny name for a Spanish author. But I had no idea why he had been able to write about exile better than anyone else. Vicente Rojo noticed my unease, and didn't wait for me to answer. By the way he had expressed himself, there was no doubt that he cared little for what I knew about Max Aub, and that he was going to say his piece no matter what.

'In 1969, Aub returned to Spain for the first time since he had left in 1939. Like many others (I'm not sure if I should include myself in this group or not), he had spent a lot of time imagining the moment when at last he would return to Spain, after the dictator had died. Well, Aub had in fact killed him in his novels. In any case, his "visit" (like the way you refer to my "visit" here in this city) went terribly, it was a total car-crash. You should read his books. Everyone should read *The Blind Chicken*. Through it you feel the terrible experience of reencountering a country he was forced to abandon thirty years ago, a country filled with old people who were once his friends, back when they were all young. Max Aub arrived in a country full of bitter old men, but that was exactly what they called him, in this country beyond repair. He also went to classes and meetings where the students "didn't have a clue who I was", as he used to say, but still believed themselves to be terribly modern. No one cared about why he'd had to leave, let alone what he'd done, said, or written for thirty years in such a far-flung place as Mexico. The students and teachers were consumed with other things; they felt so modern in a country enchanted by its own development. As modern as the teachers at your daughter's school. Many students saw Max Aub as a kind of ghost who had come from another world, another country. Mexico was very far away, and had nothing of interest for the students, who were all so smart. Do you think, then, that anybody would be interested in what I have to say to them?'

He paused, as if waiting for an answer he didn't really want to hear, and I was unable to speak, so I looked away and began to glance over the studio again. I noticed a detail I'd missed upon entering: a large painting was resting against the wall, turned inward so I couldn't see what it looked like. I was surprised that I had missed it when I walked in, because it was the first time — apart from the pencil he was holding now — that I had seen an object that reminded me of his devotion. Vicente Rojo was speaking again, this time in a confused and agitated way, about his exiled friend.

'Max Aub wrote somewhere that art is about turning truth into lies in such a way that it can remain true. I suppose he said that as Jusep Torres Campalans. I imagine you've never heard of him either, am I right?'

I shook my head gently, even though the name was dimly familiar.

'Max Aub had incurable graphomania. He wrote so much and had such a lively imagination and creative impulse that being just one writer wasn't enough. So, he invented Jusep Torres Campalans, and then he could be a painter as well. Everyone thought that Master Campalans truly existed, that he had lived in Paris and was close with Picasso, and that he had been one of the founders of Cubism. Yes, yes, everyone believed it. Why wouldn't they?' There was another pause. 'I wish you could have been at one of the salons he held on Mondays, just so you could understand what I'm trying to tell you. I could go on telling you about hundreds of other people, of the wonderful things they contributed, of the discussions we had about literature, art, journalism, how enriching those meetings were. But who could possibly care about that? Do you think your daughter's art teacher would be interested in what I have to say about exile or art?'

I felt a sharp pang: that feeling that the end of something was fast approaching. It never quite went away, and it was more like a threat than a feeling. But paradoxically, I found everything Vicente Rojo was saying very exciting — I think *exciting* is the best word for it — and a feeling of pleasure shot through my body. I could imagine myself sitting at the table at one of these salons, with that author named Max Aub, and even with the persona he invented, and I think I could also visualise the sentences in my essay about the intellectual contributions and the expansion of the mind and spirit that my fellow salon guests made possible. I would have liked to stay inside that excitement forever, inside the calm feeling that everything is fine, that nothing bad will happen, that balance is possible, and that I was close to some kind of truth. However, I still had that sharp pang of anxiety, the fear that said all of this was fleeting and would soon come to an end, and that I would never know what came next.

Perhaps this recurring sensation was nothing more than the melancholy I felt at the knowledge that this supposed balance was beyond my reach, and that the real artist I had before me could make the whole scene I had imagined disappear with a simple wave of his hand. I felt clumsy. I was twenty kilograms too heavy to imagine myself sitting at a table with intellectuals. They'd only make me seem heavier, and I'd never fit in. Maybe that's also why I was so bad at getting him to keep on talking.

'Exile is a dramatic experience, and testimonies of it can help people understand many things.' These words came from me, the fat, ungainly woman who could intuit the irritation coming from Vicente Rojo, the well-balanced man. That same woman looked away once more towards the painting resting against the wall, and then went on talking because a few words she had read somewhere or had heard at a conference happened to pop into her head at that moment. 'Rootlessness is a painful state for humans.'

'Did you say *rootlessness*? Never, ever, in my whole life have I felt rootless. Let me be clear: never. I was seventeen years old when I arrived in Mexico. My life has little in common with Max Aub's and many others. I'm a Mexican artist. Over there, I had the opportunity to work and to learn. I had the good fortune of meeting people who valued my work and helped me grow. I've said before that I am my work. I'm a Mexican artist. And the only way I achieved that was through great effort dedicated to painting and culture, which at the end of the day, are the only things worth any effort at all. I couldn't tell you anything about rootlessness. What about you, do you feel rootless?'

The fat woman (me) was surprised to be rebuked like that. Without thinking about the question, she would have immediately said yes, that of course she felt rootless. She probably did. In fact, it must have been her, because I feel much more comfortable recounting that afternoon if I distance myself from the meeting between the woman and the artist, as if it really had been another woman who once again put herself at the centre of a conversation that, when I tried to transcribe it later, filled me with embarrassment. I've already said more than once that in the essay I write about Vicente Rojo I won't leave a single mention of myself, but that other woman stole the limelight every time she met with him.

'Yes, I suppose it must be something like rootlessness. I was born in this city, but I've never felt like I belonged here. My parents are from abroad, they came to this country shortly before I was born, and they've never felt at home; it's more like they're visiting. I believe that after so many years that if they still can't fully understand the way people speak here, or if they still believe their home is abroad, it's because they were never fully welcomed. I suppose I grew up in a family that was always on the cusp of going back or moving elsewhere, even though that never quite happened. That meant that I never developed strong roots either. I've never been able to feel strongly about the customs and traditions here. I grew up surrounded by other symbols, and the language I speak is limited and flat, the bare minimum required for any daily exchange I might have with people I come across over the course of my day. In fact, I think I still believe that any day now I might move to another country. I should do it.'

'And will you do it?'

The fat woman blushed and felt overwhelmed, but she kept on talking, although with some doubt.

'I don't know. No, I don't think so. I've already told you that I've spent my whole life with this feeling that at any moment things could change, and I would leave behind all the objects and routines of my daily life. But I guess that's just the desire every person has to experience new things, to break the monotony and discover how others live in other places. Even Berta has told me that she'd like to go and live in Cádiz.'

'Fernando Pessoa said you didn't need to travel to get to know human beings. He believed that it was all in his head. One's own experiences turn into memory, which is also a form of thinking, of relating what has happened to us and who we are. So, there's not much distance between what we remember and what we imagine. Human beings make their most interesting journeys through thought and solitude. That's what Pessoa used to say.'

That last statement from Vicente Rojo unsettled the fat woman. They had arrived at one of the topics that would be important to the essay that I was trying to write: solitude. My work should offer steps for the putative reader to develop their human potential in the best way possible, avoiding moral illnesses and possible contemporary evils like rootlessness or solitude. The image of the solitary creator who knows the breadth of the world because he can travel without leaving his studio didn't match up well with another image that had come up moments ago in our conversation: the salon full of writers, painters, and journalists who seemed more cosmopolitan than exiled, as they sat around a table in a comfortable neighbourhood in Mexico. The artist kept on talking. Surprisingly, he seemed anxious to be heard, a far cry from his laconic approach in previous meetings.

'I try to protect my solitude. It's not easy. But it's essential for the work. It involves a lot of sacrifice, I won't deny that, and at times it even costs me dearly. But painting is my way of life. It's how I arrive at my truth. Writers, like Max Aub, need to create imaginary worlds, to lie and trick readers in order to arrive at reality. I don't believe that reality exists, but I do believe there is truth in the world. That's why it's so important to investigate and to work towards one's truth, the essence of being. This is what my paintings are searching for. Although I've divided them into series, they're all the same painting. I always paint the same painting; I keep going until I've found the truth inside it.'

While he spoke, he never loosened his tight grip on the pencil. Once again, I turned my gaze to the painting that was turned against the wall.

'What's more, you can only go out into the streets and

confront the world once you've done everything you need to do alone, once you've learned all the movements, gestures, and breathing of your own solitude. I suppose Pessoa meant something like that. He also used to speak of the mania caused by doubt. He said that is what characterises and determines a genius. I don't consider myself one, but the search I'm obsessed with is somewhat similar: I constantly doubt what I see, what happens, the reasons things happen. Perhaps the first thing I ever asked myself was why they took my sisters' piano away through the window. I was seven years old, and ever since then I haven't been able to stop asking myself why things happen. And I must insist, this is a search that can only be undertaken in solitude. I've known several people who have wasted all their talent and energy trying to become just like everyone else, and it has always ended badly. Groups can cause a lot of damage to individuals. We can't expect from others the things we are unable to gain ourselves. This is something we ought to learn as small children, but it doesn't always happen. I believe that the majority of people expect too much from others and too little from themselves. Don't you agree with me? If people could help us to grow without needing the recognition of others, we would be more likely to acknowledge ourselves, but in the exact meaning of the term *acknowledge*. That is to say, we could signal our talents, strengths, imagination, needs, and what we have to offer to others. Our weaknesses too, of course, but above all, they should show us the things we are capable of, our abilities and our potential. It's true that, during an essential stage of life, it's important that others — parents, siblings, teachers — show us how to recognise these things. I've already told you that my time at school was traumatic. Maybe that's why I never really cared what the teacher who tied my left hand behind my back on the first day of school expected from me.'

That same left hand lay idle in that very moment on his left thigh, while the right hand rested on the table where we had sat for all our meetings, gripping the pencil tightly. He continued his long speech. 'What I'm trying to say is that Pessoa was right. We shouldn't get carried away with things as difficult to define as the concept of "other people". Of course, some people become necessary to us. I told you before that some of the richest moments in my life were spent at those salons on Mondays. But if I told you that we were a group of people who knew how to balance our own solitude, then I wouldn't be far off the mark.'

For the fat woman listening to Vicente Rojo speak, the word *solitude* had occupied a large part of her mind over the past few months, ever since her husband told her he no longer wanted to be a part of her life. Solitude, in all these months, had consisted of not knowing what to do, of trying to control the electric tingles that she felt all over her body, and which pushed her into doing things without thinking. For the purposes of this story it doesn't matter what the woman was thinking, but the fact is, it was that same woman who was taking notes, and I doubt whether she would have been able to understand the definition of solitude offered by the artist. She hadn't chosen her solitude, and she was convinced that nothing good would come of it. Since her husband had abandoned her, her relationships with other people had become more complicated. This had even happened with her own daughter, from whom she felt increasingly distant. She had serious problems with communication. She had never felt comfortable in groups, and she had been diagnosed by more than one specialist with something like social phobia. Paradoxically, despite the diagnosis and the discomfort she felt around other people, she still hadn't found a way to be comfortable in her solitude. It was society's fault, or at least that's what she told herself. It was because of human evolution, greed, capitalism, dictatorships, the Transition, envy, totalitarianism, Nazism, gluttony, the Khmer Rouge, General Franco, nationalism, mortal sins, communism, Pinochet, centrism, idealism ... History had developed catastrophically, and when my generation came along, society was perverted and contaminated. We were asked to stop climate change (at school they showed us how to separate the rubbish to make recycling easier), but there was no certainty that we could do it.

Talking about all this with Vicente Rojo would have been very useful, because ultimately, he was going to be put on a pedestal in my essay. He probably had a few well-constructed sentences that would organise all these ideas jumbled together chaotically in the fat woman's mind. And the artist had already shown himself to be very critical of culture and education in this country. Upon reflection, it's quite probable that they did in fact discuss all this, because the woman is only capable of reflecting on these sorts of things when she is forced to because of a conversation with someone else. She knows that other people affect her — this is why she jotted 'Need for new social order' down in her notebook — but normally she considers these matters completely beyond the realm of action. When she worked as a journalist, her inability to form an opinion and make herself heard was a huge setback. Although it might appear contradictory, she failed because she was unable to voice an opinion and position herself in a profession that ought to be limited to recounting events objectively without mediating or conditioning them, contrasting them only with the words of others. This is why she sought a 'new social order', to give herself the opportunity to understand it from the outset, so that she could become involved and feel like she was part of something.

I have no doubt now that the woman spoke about all this with the artist, because in the notebook she wrote down questions that she herself could never ask. 'A new order, but different how? If you don't recognise the order/structure you are a part of (whether you like it or not), how can you know what you're looking for, given it doesn't exist? Does it really not exist, or are you just unaware of it? Or can it never exist because it responds only to a wish, a fantasy of yours, which is to say — your truth?' I'm sick of searching, even passively, and I still haven't found the place where I ought to feel comfortable in the existing order or structure. I believe that other people have not allowed me to develop. What happens to undeveloped potential? I was a smart girl with plans to do something interesting in life. In fact, I grew up thinking I had to do something worthy of the society I had grown up in. Perhaps Vicente Rojo was referring to this when he said it's important to acknowledge ourselves and come to terms with our abilities and our limits. I was convinced that I was a smart girl who could do great things, but I was always waiting for someone else to tell me how and when.

It was an afternoon with many periods of silence. Vicente Rojo made it known he wished to finish up:

'Do you think you have enough material now to write your interview? Or have you finally realised that it's not worth wasting any more time on this?'

Right now, I'm imagining the response that someone capable of refocussing the situation back to the interview would have articulated. But the woman sitting at the table in the artist's spotless studio just mumbled a few words that were barely audible when she tried to listen to them later on her recorder.

'Of course it's worth continuing. They're very interested in publishing my article in the newspaper, I've told you that already.'

'Then I'm just going to have to give you this painting and a few catalogues, where there are some splendid texts written by great friends that will be very helpful to you. Then you can go off and write your article about the only thing that matters, Vicente Rojo's oeuvre, and you can forget all about my "visit to the city", as you like to call it.'

'But are you planning on staying long? I thought you had moved here. When are you staying until?'

'I don't think anybody's interested in that, believe me. It's getting late, and you have a charming daughter waiting for you at home, so I think it would be best if we left our chat at that. Don't you agree?'

The woman is confused. There are still many topics they haven't discussed. In some of the articles she's read online, critics described Vicente Rojo's paintings as full of vibrations. When she read those articles, she finally understood what she'd once been taught about light and colour being vibrations. But she has doubts over what all that material means. She likes to think that while she converses with the man before her, nothing bad can happen. It's as if she could live through him and his words, as if she could become a part of the artist's life, as if some small part of everything he has said had actually happened to her.

She tells the artist that, obviously, she doesn't wish to disturb him any longer, that she's taken advantage of his generosity, but that she can't quite wrap up the interview without asking a final question that she considers transcendental.

'You haven't disturbed me, but I do think we've spoken too much. If you insist, I have no problems answering a final question, but we do need to wrap things up.'

The woman poses her question:

'Many critics claim your paintings feature the vibrations of material. What do you make of that? How would you define material?'

The artist clears his throat and sighs. He gives the woman a tired look, and after a few moments, begins talking once more. Each time she poses a question, he considers his response before answering, so that he can build a logical discourse of sentences with beginnings and endings that form coherent statements. Vicente Rojo answers the final question, but the fat woman is no longer listening. I don't remember what he said, but in the notebook there are statements I will have to rely upon not only for the article about the artist, but also for the essay I want to write. There's also the recording of the conversation, but I'm too embarrassed to listen to it, so I'm just counting on the disparate and sometimes unintelligible comments I wrote.

The artist answered my question about material. He said that in effect, he was interested in how painting could cease to be merely a vehicle for expressing meaning, and become an object in itself. Painting in itself. The artist no longer wishes to copy from the reality he sees, but instead wishes to create a new reality, one that would be much truer. He said that no one could explain this better than his friend Juan García Ponce. Painting, with its textures and volume, could become a volcano, a desert, rain falling over a landscape. This is how it can produce an absolute identification between what is seen, what can be perceived by the other senses, and other invisible truths. The purpose (the responsibility) of an artist is to place a hitherto hidden truth in front of the eyes of the beholder. Material is reality, but each person perceives it differently. Everything is material. We are material, and even schoolchildren know (maybe the students at my daughter's school didn't know, nor those who have never heard the name Max Aub) that material can never be destroyed. It remains, because it is eternal. It simply changes. It changes in Vicente Rojo's paintings: always the same painting, always so different and surprising. It's always the same material. This is why death does not exist, it's simply one more transformation.

According to my notebook, the Mexican artist stated that following death, human beings go on existing in a different form. Material cannot be destroyed, but it can be scattered, like pollen. It can dissipate, like a fog that slowly clears instead of simply disappearing, dividing itself into multiple particles that end up in the most unsuspected places, some that are invisible to our eyes, because they travel through the other side of the looking-glass and no one has shown us how to see them.

This is why in his work he seeks the elemental forms: circles, squares, lines. The meaning of everything, from across all of time, can be found in these forms: that which links us to our most truthful essence, that which reminds us we are merely material that has been melted down then fused with more material, which can manifest itself in infinite forms.

Finally, we brought the interview to a close. I was far from satisfied with the results. I could no longer see the shapes of the paragraphs of my article in my head. I could no longer imagine the lines of my text having the same harmony and flourish as the lines with which Vicente Rojo had reproduced the rain over Mexico in his paintings. So, I knew that without a doubt I'd got myself into a real mess. Again.

The artist must have sensed my despair, and, maybe to console me, he insisted that I accept his painting as a gift. He also gave me the books and catalogues about his oeuvre that he had mentioned earlier. They'd all be very useful for my writing, but the situation seemed a little over the top, because of his generosity, the size of the painting, and my discomfort. I knew he was getting rid of something valuable, of objects that were almost like talismans for him, like the pencil he'd held on to throughout the whole interview.

My discomfort only grew on the journey home. I could even say that I finally understood the rejection Berta was compelled to when faced by that man and his generosity. I remember moving the painting from his studio to my house as something so out of proportion it was almost grotesque. In his hurry for me to take the painting and leave his studio, I hadn't even had time to look at it, and I felt something like shame when we passed people staring at us in the street. I thought that it was no way to transport a painting by Vicente Rojo, and that there was something worrying about how anxious he was to get rid of his own artwork.

Because of the way our last interview had gone, I had no doubt that he would never invite me to his studio again. I'd given up on the possibility of another interview altogether. I already had several hours of conversation recorded, and I could lean on everything that had been written about him by others.

Carrying the painting home was such an onerous task, with so many difficulties along the way, that the easiest thing would have been to give up. But we didn't. In silence, except for the bare minimum to coordinate our movements, the artist and I did our best to work our way around all the different angles in the three flights of stairs we had to climb. We were both irritated. Between the first and second floors a bit of wood snapped off the frame, which made the absurdity of the situation even more intense. But even that wasn't enough to stop us. We kept at it until a painting about two metres tall by three metres wide with the entire right side of the frame ruined made it through the door of my apartment. As soon as I was inside with the painting, Vicente Rojo very discreetly said goodbye and set off. I left his artwork resting against the wall in the hallway.

Berta arrived home a few hours later. I had been so bewildered by the way the last interview had gone and the process of transporting the painting that I hadn't even thought of my daughter's possible reaction when she saw it in our home.

She came into the study where I was taking refuge, perhaps to remind myself that all these crazy happenings served a purpose: I intended to write an article and an essay about a Mexican artist whose work and ethics were a kind of beacon. I was trying to organise all the notes I had taken. Berta watched me and waited a few seconds before speaking. She was in a bad mood.

'I can't have a pet, but you've bought yourself a huge, horrible painting.'

'I didn't buy it. It's a painting by Vicente Rojo, although you'd never understand what that means. And anyway, there's no reason why you can't have a pet.'

'Oh really? I can have one now?'

'Berta, I never said you couldn't have a pet. You've just become obsessed with an impossible option because the ibis, in addition to being practically extinct, is a bird that cannot live inside an apartment. Do you want to argue about this again?'

She was having trouble breathing, and her eyes were wet and shiny. Any other mother would have understood that she should get to the bottom of what was making her daughter upset, but I was afraid and I lived under the constant threat that a tragedy might take place. And I was feeling unsettled myself.

'Why did you bring that painting home?'

In the beginning, it seemed like she was going to continue talking, but instead she burst into tears and shut herself in her bedroom. Berta is a nervous crier. Ever since she was small, whenever she couldn't contain her own sense of discomfort, ridiculousness, or rage, she has erupted into nervous weeping that tightens her throat and prevents her from talking. It had often frightened me, because she would then break out into a raspy coughing fit that was so loud and hoarse it was hard to believe it came from such a tiny, fragile body. It's hair-raising to hear her cry like that. Pablo always blamed me for bringing on these fits. Sometimes they were so loud that they shook the walls, and that's no exaggeration. As she grew up, the coughing grew even stronger. When she cries like that, I'm always afraid that something inside her will break. That night she cried for quite some time. It was obvious that I should have gone into her room to try to calm her down, but I reacted too late. When at last I went in, she didn't reject my embrace, despite what I was expecting, but instead let me hold her in my arms. That's how I experienced it: a slight relaxation in her muscles in which she let go of the strength and effort required to keep her body upright. She had given in and abandoned herself. She had capitulated in the face of something much greater than her, something I had no idea about. When at last she had calmed down, we were able to talk.

When Berta was four or five years old and had one of these attacks, I would become alarmed to the point where reality disappeared and the only thing that truly mattered was making sure my daughter was breathing, that she wasn't coughing up blood, that she was OK. A sick child is a painful contradiction in terms. Something like a paradox that reminds us not only of the fragility of existence, but that everything is the fruit of chance, that destiny is arbitrary, because the normal, logical thing would be for a child to grow up, go to school, enter society, and relieve the preceding generation from their posts, even if we never understand the purpose or meaning of this whole chain of people replacing one another. But this is the logic of the world we live in, and the basis from which we build everything else. And this logic had been overthrown for my daughter. That night, when she managed to stop crying and her breathing became normal again, she told me that for several months she had been playing the prosopagnosia game — which I already knew about — the game where she stared into the mirror while holding her breath for so long that either she could no longer recognise her own face or she had beaten the other players. She always played with Mario and Lucas, and she almost always won, because Lucas got bored quickly (in fact, he didn't even like the game) and Mario fainted more easily than she did. I remembered that I still had to take her to the doctor to discuss these fainting spells and for her to have a general examination. Berta kept on talking, as if she needed to explain something that she herself couldn't understand. She needed to reconstruct her story to find any small details she had passed over. During one of these fainting spells, Mario had hit his head against the sink in the boys' bathroom and bled profusely from his jaw. This is why the teacher had called in the parents of all three children. Mario's mother had been very frightened because Mario needed six stitches, and he was taken to the doctor to discuss his fainting. I felt guilty for not having done that yet. The doctors said that Mario had a terrible illness, one of those ones that tend to be suffered by old people rather than children. When a fifteen-year-old boy receives a diagnosis like that, it becomes a tragic contradiction in terms.

Berta said that Mario had told them that there was a positive side to his illness: he could get out of most of his classes, and skip the exams. Although she didn't know how to put it into words, I think her friend's joke had moved her. I felt a calmness in her story that surprised me. Yes, I had heard her terrible nervous crying, but after that she was talking to me in order to convince herself that she could overcome a situation that was clearly too much for her. Words would give shape to what was happening. Words like *chemotherapy, operation, radiation,* or *transplant* seemed out of place in a conversation with my daughter, who was only fifteen years old. It was made even more strange, because these words were mixed with others like *report cards, homework, exams, end-of-year trip, holidays.* While she spoke, the situation she described existed as a purely semantic problem, until Berta said something like 'I don't want to die,' and then hugged me.

I can't remember exactly when my daughter discovered death. Perhaps it's something she discussed with her father. Pablo knew it was one of the things I was most afraid of in motherhood: the day I would have to explain to my daughter that death was a part of life, and that it is inevitable. Perhaps he was the one who told her about Heaven, because it was an idea she absorbed from a very young age in her conception of the world and existence. I had never been in a situation where I had to comfort her, until then.

I would have liked to have been able to calm her, but I couldn't think of anything better to say than that death was a long way off, that life was long, that she was just a kid, and that there were still many wonderful things that would happen in her life, so there was no point in thinking about death because right now it made no sense. Besides, Mario wasn't dead, he was just sick, and there were advanced treatments available that could cure illnesses like his. My arguments seemed weak even to myself. I tried to reconstruct everything the artist had told me about material and its resilience, but it was no good, I couldn't even find a way to begin. But Berta listened to me and seemed calmer. Perhaps all she needed was to express her anxiety to someone and hear a soothing voice, regardless of what that voice was saying. My daughter was too smart to be comforted by the sort of banal things I'd been saying to her.

After a while, she began to speak again. She said she couldn't imagine living without Mario, that it was thanks to him and Lucas that she made it through the day at school. She said Lucas was an idiot for not listening to Mario when he told them about his sickness, and that afterwards he'd acted like nothing had happened and everything was still the same. Berta said that a world without Mario would be a much worse place. I told her again that it's possible to fight illnesses, that there are effective treatments that cure them, that I had read somewhere that in seventy-five per cent of cases the illness becomes chronic, which is to say that it will still be there, but it will be stable. Berta let me speak, but when she picked up her train of thought again it was exactly the same as before I had interrupted her. A world without Mario would be much worse because he was one of those people who never gets angry and because he always did whatever he could to ensure other people had a good time. Then she said she didn't understand why the illness had to affect him, seeing as it was *her* lot to suffer the ugliest, most terrible things in life. But when she looked at it properly, it did make sense, because in the end she would be the one who had to witness her best friend's death, after which she would be stuck with Lucas, who was an idiot. So, she would suffer the worst after all. She had seen plenty of films and she thought she knew how things would go from here. What she meant was, she shouldn't be surprised, because this was her destiny. I tried to interrupt her a couple of times, but she didn't want to hear my arguments again. I thought I'd have to seek help from some kind of therapist. Maybe at the school, if they were already aware of Mario's illness, they had thought about making some kind of counselling available to the students. While I was thinking about all of this, my daughter kept sobbing in my arms. She had begun crying again, this time without the nervous coughing, and at times it was difficult to follow what she was saying, but I was able to understand that she was sick of everyone trying to deceive her: teachers, classmates, her father, me ... Her father and I had betrayed her, or something like that.

She also told me she didn't understand why I had accepted those gifts from the painter. She wished he hadn't helped her get home on the day she fainted. She'd never asked for it. She had fainted in front of the painting because she wanted to see its enormous size in three dimensions. Earlier that afternoon, in the boys' bathroom, Mario had beaten her in one of their breath-holding contests. But this time it hadn't been in front of a mirror, but while they stared at an illustration given to them by their psychology teacher so that they could try to see images in three dimensions. Mario was feeling smug because he *had* seen it in three dimensions and had been able to hold his breath the longest. So, when Berta saw that painting in the foyer, composed of cubes and figures in relief, she was reminded of the psychology teacher's illustration, and she couldn't help staring at it. She also told me that while she was staring at the painting, just before she fainted, she saw something in it that frightened her, but she didn't know how to explain it. It was just a game, and that's why she couldn't understand all this carry-on with the painter. The painting wasn't beautiful. Even so, it wasn't ugly enough to form part of the ugliness of her surroundings. It was just a painting that no longer interested her, and then all of a sudden, her mother had become obsessed with going and interviewing the painter and filling their house with his artworks. She didn't want to see them; they weren't the kind of ugly things that made her feel better. Only truly horrendous things belonged in her world, things that turn the stomachs of those who behold them, because it reminds them that the world is not perfect, that terrible things happen, like a fifteen-year-old boy suffering from cancer, or how when your parents separate, your life is turned upside down, and it feels like the entire world is spinning backwards.

'Would we be able to tell if the world was spinning backwards? It's true that we can't tell that the world is constantly spinning, but I'm sure that if the world suddenly started spinning the other way, we'd notice. When Dad lived here, we didn't realise that was "normal" — we only realised that after he left, right?'

This wasn't a question to which she expected an answer. I just wanted to hug her, to keep listening to her.

'Don't you see how great it would be to have an ibis in the apartment?'

I remembered my dream with the bird carrying a stack of papers covered with Berta's tiny circles in its beak, stalking through the hallway, where Vicente Rojo's painting now rested against the wall.

'You're right. We should get one.'

PART 2

THE MAN WHO THOUGHT HE WAS VICENTE ROJO

Not long after I finished my degree, I began working at a publishing house that put out encyclopaedias. I wasn't sure if this was something I was passionate about or had always dreamed of doing. But, if I'm honest, I did feel lucky to have been chosen. Sometimes, when I tell my daughter about that experience, she breaks into hysterical fits of laughter. She can't understand the importance of an encyclopaedia, because since she was born, it has been possible to type a question into Google whenever you want to know anything. But I grew up in a house where one of the walls in the dining room was covered with a bookshelf full of encyclopaedias that were so specific, I'm not sure if any of my siblings ever consulted them. My favourite was the one that covered the major events of World War II: in each of the volumes there was an appendix that included reproductions of all the front pages of Spanish and European newspapers as they broke the news of those earth-shattering events. What I liked most was looking at those front pages, especially from the European newspapers, in languages I couldn't understand, but which I knew spoke of the war.

I'm not trying to say that this is where my calling as a journalist came from. In fact, I doubt I ever really had a calling for it. I think I decided to study Communication Sciences because during my last year of high school — back then it was called the University Orientation Course — my art history teacher came in before class and dropped a newspaper clipping on my desk. It was a summary of a speech where Gabriel García Márquez had declared that journalism was the best profession in the world. Just like that, he'd given the writer a headline for his article. I'd never even read a book by Gabriel García Márquez, but I liked my art history teacher's sensibilities; in class he'd shown us Botticelli's *The Birth of Venus* and *Primavera*. Thinking about it now, it occurs to me how funny it would be if the teacher had left it on my desk accidentally.

When I began working at the publishing house, I'd already been writing for a local newspaper for a few months. They sent me to cover press conferences given by the mayor, and even sometimes to openings and events attended by some important regional politician. I won't deny that I enjoyed being entrusted with such a duty: I became the only person responsible for recounting these events to the newspaper's thousands of readers. Once, I accidentally changed the name or job title of one those regional authorities, a fact that was later relayed to me by the editors. But it was no big deal for them, because at the end of the day, I was still learning.

The culture section was my favourite, and my goal was to write for the weekend lift-out. Occasionally, writers or intellectuals would come by the offices, and spend time chatting with the editors. I listened in on their conversations about new literary titles, recent exhibits, and current trends in philosophy. All of these overheard conversations had an effect on my mood, but I was especially moved when I recognised a name that was mentioned. That was when I confused who I wanted to be with who I actually was: a girl who had just received an official piece of paper saying she had been awarded her degree, but who actually thought the paper said that the moment had arrived where everyone would recognise her value, because she had always been such a clever girl. By eavesdropping on the intellectuals who came to visit the local newspaper, I thought of myself as their equal. I felt I was just like them, even though they would never have recognised me as such, (I would never have recognised myself as such, either) because I had no idea who I was, let alone who I wanted to be. But I also wanted to try acting like one of those people who knows so much about so many things that everything becomes completely unbearable, because all that knowledge can only lead to an essentially negative truth.

My first boss at the publishing house didn't seem particularly inclined to acknowledge how clever I was either. She gave me one of the worst tongue-lashings I've ever received in my life. After all this time I can't remember exactly what she said, just the modulation of her tirade, the melody of her intonation as she spoke, how she bit off each of her words and tightened her jaw, which was a move I'd only ever seen from actors in old Western movies. She made me aware of the gravity of taking things for granted in a job like the one I was supposed to be doing. You could never trust others to know what you knew, you had to confirm and double-check everything — wasn't I a journalist? Hadn't anyone explained to me how important it was to check your information? Nothing should be taken as a given until you had verified it from trustworthy sources. All this to say that if I had any doubts, I should talk to her about them, because she'd be happy to help me out, just like she was right now.

It's possible that my constant fear of making a mistake stems from this experience. I also think that my feeling of living near to the end of things grew stronger in this period. Although I had no idea at the time, encyclopaedias as I knew them had very little time left on Earth. Even my mother was soon in a rush to get rid of all the books she had covering the shelves, even the ones with the reproductions of the front pages of newspapers from World War II.

My job at the publishing house didn't last much longer, so I went back to writing for the regional newspaper. One Friday, they called me up at my parents' house to ask if I could cover a conference given by a very popular philosopher that afternoon in the region's capital. None of the usual reporters were available, so if I could go, it would be a huge favour. I was delighted to accept. That's when the editor of the culture section's weekend lift-out asked me to try to interview the philosopher for a lead article. At last, the moment had arrived when everyone would realise how clever I was. Of course, I told him, I'll get you that interview. I got in touch with the conference organisers and they assured me that there'd be no problem. As long as it was brief, I could interview the philosopher before he gave his speech, because once that was over, he had to leave straight away for another engagement. I promised them it would be a brief interview, just the minimum I needed to put together the article.

A taxi deposited the philosopher in front of the cultural centre where he would be giving his speech fifteen minutes after the time he was supposed to have begun. Obviously, there was no way I'd be able to interview him. The auditorium was packed with people impatient to hear the philosopher's advice. Although I was supposed to write a story on what he said, I was barely able to follow it. I was angry and bewildered. I felt completely incapable of telling the editor of the culture section that I had been unable to secure an interview with one of the most sought-after intellectuals in the region. During his conference, I think he advised his readers and admirers to be respectful towards others, to live together in harmony, and to want what you already have, because that way, you have what you want. He said we should apply the principles of the Enlightenment to our lives, enjoy sunny mornings and rainy afternoons: in short, we should be happy. How did my failure that afternoon fit in with his advice?

After what seemed like endless rounds of applause, his speech was finally over. I approached the conference organisers to see if I couldn't get a couple of minutes with the philosopher. But it was impossible: he had to return immediately to the judges' meeting for a very important philosophy prize. I managed to make my way over to him, but he just looked at me with his squinty eyes and said with forced friendliness that a taxi was already waiting for him. Without thinking, I suggested we could do the interview in the taxi, and that's what happened.

This is the best anecdote I have from my time as a journalist, and it's also the most daring I've ever been in a professional setting. I can't recall the content of the interview, but I do remember that the taxi driver wanted to charge me for the return trip, after we had dropped the philosopher off at the famous restaurant where the other jury members were meeting. I didn't pay him.

As an anecdote, it had a certain charm, and it caused the editor of the culture section to call me up and praise me for my quick thinking, and to insist that I include it at the start of the interview. I think I felt something like happiness when I saw it in print, in the middle pages of the weekend lift-out. At last, I had entered into the decisive phase of my life, where everyone would recognise my talent. I imagined myself sitting face to face with the editor, discussing philosophy and current trends in contemporary thought, about the need to appreciate what one has, as it's the only way to ensure one has what one wants, about the need for ethical guidelines to make it possible for humans to live harmoniously together, and how that was the only way to fill the void left by postmodernism. I listened to the sound of my speech without noticing the words or the language in which I pronounced it, like the incomprehensible spiels delivered by characters in Charlie Chaplin films, after he finally allowed the use of sound.

A few days after the interview was published, I returned to the newspaper's offices and went to over to greet the editor of the culture section. He was friendly, and he congratulated me on my work. We spoke superficially for a few minutes about the philosopher's theories as shown by his responses in the interview. When we seemed to have run out of things to say on that topic, I told him that now that I'd started writing for the culture section, I wanted to keep doing so, and that he should assign me more projects. By the way he looked at me — a smile that couldn't quite hide a feeling of awkward surprise — I realised I'd done the wrong thing. Maybe the door to the next successful phase of my professional life wasn't open after all. 'OK, propose some projects, pitch some articles, and I'll take a look at them.' He hadn't even finished his sentence when a regular contributor to the culture section approached, a man I'd overheard discussing Schopenhauer on many occasions.

The editor introduced us. He told the regular contributor that I was the author of the interview with the philosopher that had been published in the latest edition. 'Ah,' was the only response from the contributor. When the editor asked him what he had thought of it, the contributor began a long speech that I found difficult to follow, and which reminded me a lot of my boss's diatribes at the publishing company. From the Schopenhauer specialist's sermon all I retained was that one should be very careful when writing down philosophers' names, and that it's essential to double-check facts before accepting them as true, and, needless to say, before publishing them.

End result: all the happiness and pride I felt at the publication of the interview quickly evaporated. So, when the editor of a different culture section — this time from the capital city of the region — called me a few days later, I was certain it was to chastise me for something I'd written in the interview. I was certain that I'd done something wrong and I'd grossly offended someone. But he spoke to me in a friendly manner and let me know that he'd heard how I managed to sneak into the philosopher's taxi, and that he'd read my interview. He was interested in meeting me. As you can imagine, that's when I heard the hinges squeak as the doors to success and recognition finally opened for me.

At our first meeting, the editor of the culture section at the newspaper in the region's capital wanted to know about my education and work experience. I told him about the publishing house and the regional newspaper. Then he asked me lots of questions about the interview in the taxi. Once more I repeated my spiel about wanting what you have so you can have what you want, the ethical guidelines for harmonious relations between neighbours which will allow human beings to overcome the existential void and the certainty of civilisation's doom. Obviously, he was evaluating my knowledge, so he wore a look of genuine interest, and I held forth with the self-assured manner of someone who is sure she has arrived at the highest planes of privilege, where a position has been waiting for her for some time.

He told me that over the past few months, several publishing houses had been putting out books of accessible philosophy. I didn't want to think about what the Schopenhauer expert might have thought about my article on the popular philosopher, because I was already considering writing something that would inform potential readers about these new philosophy titles. The editor of the culture section at the regional capital's newspaper seemed pleased, because he promised more assignments in the near future.

I ended up finding out what the Schopenhauer expert thought anyway, because one afternoon I bumped into him again at the offices of the regional newspaper. On that occasion, it was he who approached me at my workstation, and, without any preamble at all, he began talking to me about epigones — a word whose meaning was unknown to me at the time — and frivolous commercial projects. The only argument I could raise in my defence was that I was just trying to spread the word about newly published books, but that didn't convince him. I heard the words *epigone* and *frivolous* all over again. When he left, I noticed that the editor of the culture section of the regional newspaper had a smug smile on his face.

The times I was told off by my boss at the publishing house and the Schopenhauer expert melded in my mind and tortured me in endless nightmares while I slept, then swirled in my mind all day long. I lived in fear of all those words, and I heard them echoing so loudly in my head that I was convinced that if somebody got close enough — on the bus, for example — they'd be able to hear the voices of those two people shouting about how ignorant I was and how incapable of writing anything with the slightest amount of rigour. When I met someone in the street, I could only imagine what that person thought of me, because I already knew that I was completely incapable of getting anything done properly. At night, in that intermediary zone between wakefulness and sleep, I imagined how quickly my life would be ruined when my bosses at both newspapers, and the journalists who worked there, told everyone how incapable I was of doing anything worthwhile. My life would soon come to an end, because even Pablo, whom I had been seeing for several years at that stage and who had professed unconditional love for me, would surely leave.

Despite everything, I was given more assignments, for both newspapers. I had to learn how to walk around the offices without my legs trembling and without constantly blushing. I had to stay very alert, because I knew that at any moment they might spring a trap on me that would reveal without doubt how farcical the life I was attempting to lead really was. There was no room in journalism for people like me. For a time, I was getting regular work, and I flitted between the happiness I felt at each assignment (of course I never dared to pitch anything myself, I was too afraid of everything) and the terror I felt whenever I turned something in. The night before one of my pieces was to be published, I could barely sleep, and when I finally drifted off I had nightmares about the terrible mistakes I had made in my articles. There was no point going over it a thousand times before submitting, there would always be an error or a typo. It got so that I had doubts over the meaning and spelling of the simplest words and even over my own mental health. I wondered if I'd contracted some kind of illness where my brain no longer sent information correctly to my hands or mouth when I wrote or spoke.

The long-awaited day when my life would end because everyone discovered how hopeless I was never arrived. Or maybe it did arrive, and it was just much subtler than I had imagined. Pablo passed his public exams and to celebrate, he asked me to move in with him, which I did. More time passed and Berta was born, then someone told Pablo that an insurance company was looking for someone trained in communications for a job in their press department. We both agreed that this would provide much-needed stability, given that we had just started a family. Every time I sent a press release or made a call, my whole body shook, but I learned to live with it.

Although the time between each article in the newspapers grew longer and longer, I never pulled away fully, especially from the newspaper in the regional capital. But the regional newspaper folded not long after I went to live with Pablo. Which is all to say, that in a certain sense, I actually *was* close to the end of something, the whole time I worked there. Isabel had risen to become editor in chief of the newspaper in the regional capital, and we had remained friendly. We kept on running into each other and making dinner dates we never kept. Even so, she was still my closest, most concrete connection with the newspaper. When I called her to pitch the interview with Vicente Rojo, I knew she was pleased and surprised in equal parts. Later on, the idea that we could scoop the other newspapers over the artist's visit had excited her enough to encourage me to write something, anything, and soon, even though I wasn't used to writing things like that.

I had one of Vicente Rojo's massive paintings, with a broken frame, sitting in the hallway of my apartment. My daughter had told me that the art teacher in the neighbourhood high school had not allowed him to give lessons there. I had recorded several long conversations with him during which I had gathered barely any material for the article the newspaper wanted. I hadn't even been able to determine whether it would be an interview, a profile, or a feature. It had changed from being the article I wanted to write into something I was being asked to do, and once again, I wasn't sure if I'd be able to do it.

I still felt enough of my original excitement to think it was a good idea for the newspaper in the capital to publish something written by me about Vicente Rojo, but other, more vague anxieties were beginning to take hold of my brain. You could say I had forgotten the reasons why I wanted to write about the artist in the first place. Perhaps what I was trying to do was capture the melody I thought I could hear while he spoke, the melody that had washed over me like a revelation, an epiphany that demanded some sort of reaction. I still believe that when something like this happens to a person, they are obliged to leave evidence of it, but I have serious doubts about whether I'd be the best person for such a situation. I'd read on many occasions that music is the purest aesthetic expression, because it translates directly to emotion. From these givens, I reason that I was trying to come up with a formula, the correct combination of sounds from the artist's message that had momentarily created a balanced world. I felt obliged to write about all this, which was another way of deciphering the mystery — as if I were capable of finding words to describe and bring forth the same effect as music — so that I could remember it whenever necessary.

This whole theory might seem outlandish, but the fact remains that I hadn't thought of writing all these revelations from the artist down in a personal diary or one of my many notebooks. Instead, I had planned to publish them in an article in the newspaper from the provincial capital. So, at a bare minimum, this desire indicated that this was something beyond the scope of things that normally made me stop and think. But people don't stop to think about all the things they should; in fact, in my case, during the period when I met Vicente Rojo, I had a clear tendency to think a lot less than a human being should. One thing I have no doubt about is that throughout those months, I fantasised about a woman capable of writing an article about Vicente Rojo and all his truths — where his greatness came from, the precise nature of the state of ecstasy provoked by his artworks — and, above all, I believed that that woman could be me, even if I *was* twenty kilos too heavy. At a time when the rules that had governed my reality were changing in an alarming way, I needed to believe that I was someone capable of writing a good article about this painter who by chance had entered into my life. I would also have the opportunity to tell a good story, the kind that shows the essence of a human being as they achieve their full potential, as their energies and multiple ways of being synergise. And it had to be a story published in print, because that was its natural medium. Newspapers were invented to leave written proof of significant events, to explain to readers how the world works, and to expand one's horizons. It was also the ideal medium for me, because it seemed like printed newspapers, too, were entering their final phase. Many visionaries said that print's days were numbered, and that newspapers would soon disappear. Nobody I knew in those days went to a newsstand to buy a newspaper; they didn't even read them in the bars where you could still find them on the counter. But I wanted my piece on Vicente Rojo to be published in the newspaper from the regional capital: just like the artist, perhaps I, too, had come to believe that the internet didn't exist.

Asking myself why I wanted to write the damn article was, without a doubt, a very pertinent question. But it's also true that Isabel kept on hounding me for the article, and the painful truth of the situation was that I didn't have enough material to write anything. I'd left the books and catalogues that the artist had given me next to the computer, on the desk that for so long was occupied exclusively by Pablo. Vicente Rojo had told me himself that I would find all my answers in those pages. I began with the most recent one, *Open Diary*, which was a book so exquisite that, without exaggeration, I was deeply moved simply by touching its pages. I was surprised to find many paragraphs underlined, as if Vicente Rojo himself had wished to draw my attention to the matters he considered most important. The artist wasn't lying when he gave me the book: it was all here. As I read the underlined fragments, I heard the musicality of his voice again. All I needed to do was put the puzzle pieces he had laid out for me together: 'the first memory I have took place on July 19, 1936, when I was four years old. I have a vivid recollection of the reaction in Barcelona to Franco's uprising. I saw the whole thing from the window of my home. [...] Ever since then, the awareness that joy is inseparable from sorrow has structured my work (and my life).'

There are other quotes and passages: some that speak of a double childhood, one about that boy staring out the window on July 19, 1936 and one about an adolescent whose life lights up once he arrives in Mexico; passages about the boy who has his left hand tied behind his back at school, and passages about a young artist questioning his creative impulses: 'At the origin of each of my artistic projects there is the need to fill a void, and my true, abiding interest has been in figuring out how to do it. There has also been an artist's desire to become someone else: I decided to depersonalise myself and invent a new painter (who unfortunately has to be called Vicente Rojo, too).'

This last fragment reminded me that the previous night I had dreamt that at last all my efforts had come into fruition, and I had become someone else. Far from living through a painful process of metamorphosis, in my dream I was already a different person who could look down on the insecure, timid, and fat woman who was disappearing as easily as a 'fade-to-black' effect on TV. The fact that I had managed to dream something so audio-visual was in itself a sign that I had already become someone else. I know it doesn't mean anything, that it's a very common feeling, and that when Vicente Rojo spoke of his desire to become a different painter he wasn't talking about what I'd experienced, but a much more complex creative search, but for me the coincidence was something worth keeping in mind.

Advancing through Vicente Rojo's book, I came across a text about a Catalan man from Mollerussa named Jusep Torres Campalans and his arrival in Chiapas in 1915. Vicente Rojo had told me about this in one of our meetings. I knew that name was linked to a certain game or puzzle concerning what was real, what was realistic, and what was true. In his text, Vicente Rojo attributed to Torres Campalans the idea that 'art is converting truth into lies so that it never stops being true' and the creation of a splendid book called *Max Aub: The Novel*. On that very page in the book, he had taped a piece of paper with something that looked like a quote or an aphorism by 'Jusep Torres Campalans.' The note said, 'Blend yourself with your work. Be your own work. Don't look at yourself from the outside. Never step back from the canvas to see the aspect of the brushstrokes. Be so inside that you cannot step outside what you have done. Nothing is worth anything, especially not a finished work. At the end of the day, it's all rubbish.'

How would I ever be able to write a feature for the newspaper based on these riddles? The assumed reader of my article would be reading it to share in the revelations supposedly gained by local high school students after receiving classes from a prestigious artist who had come home after many years of exile: the nephew of a heroic soldier who, despite everything, had been defeated. Thanks to this legacy, the kids would hear the testimony of someone who represented the nation's dramatic history, the richness and exoticism of many years in Mexico, the patina of a renowned intellectual with whom powerful politicians from all over the world had wanted to have their photos taken, and the humility of an artist who returned to his homeland because he had never been able to forget the essential things: roots and childhood. But from the clues I'd been able to gather myself, I'd never be able to write the article. Where did that huge painting sitting in my hallway fit into all this?

I had caught Berta staring at the painting on several occasions. Since Mario's diagnosis, a calm had settled over us. She still maintained a certain distance from me, which she seemed to be using to protect herself, but she was much less tense, and she was distracted by other matters that were much more important than everyday skirmishes caused by living with me. She never tried to hide it when I found her looking at the painting. Even so, I knew better than to ask. Finally, it was Berta herself who wanted to talk about it.

'I always used to tell Mario and Jorge that you have to look from behind the eyes, straight from the optic nerve, because the image that arrives at the brain is composed inside the eye. Only if you look directly from the brain are you able to perceive an object's pure form. That way you can see things in different ways, without them being what we've always been told they are. Which is to say that if you see a door or a landscape, that's because ever since you were small you've been told that it's a door or a landscape. But if you're able to see the colours and forms separately, without a small part of your brain telling you "this is a landscape," the reality is quite different. This is why you have to try to see things with your brain. I think that if you try a little harder, you can even see things that are not normally there. Do you think so?'

'That's the game you used play at school, isn't it?'

'Since Mario got sick we don't play it anymore, but I still try it sometimes. If there are ultra-violet rays or insects or bacteria we can't see, then there have to be other things our eyes can't see, right? We should learn to perceive these things in other ways. Dogs, for example, can hear and smell things that we can't.'

'I don't think Mario's illness has anything to do with this.'

I wasn't trying to reassure Berta, I was simply telling her what I thought. But I had a feeling she interpreted my words as interference, and I understood I wasn't allowed to talk about her game. She kept looking at the painting.

'It's important to hold your breath, because breathing controls the rhythm of the circulation of blood as it flows to the brain, and the brain tells us how we should see everything. While you breathe, everything is normal, and the body functions just the same as always, so you can't force it to see things differently. It's like when you manage to see an image in three dimensions. That day I was trying to see the painting in three dimensions, which is why I fainted, because I saw an image that frightened me, as if I were floating in the air and about to fall down amongst all those blocks, like in a dream when you fall from a precipice.'

I never saw blocks in the sequences of squares and cubes of different colours that made up the painting, but I couldn't tell her that. Berta continued talking:

'When you manage to see things from behind your eyes, or with your whole brain, everything is different. In our literature class, we had to read a story by Cristina Fernández Cubas where she explains this whole thing. It's about a boy who learns to see everything through the lens of horror, and then he can't stand anything at all. It's a scary story, and it doesn't end well. Something similar is happening to me now, I can no longer see things the way you do, or the way others do. You can't see what's terrifying about this painting, which is why you interview that man and go to see him at his house.'

Berta's reference to the writer reminded me of something Vicente Rojo had mentioned: the painter Bram van Velde's comment that 'once the eye has confronted horror, it sees it everywhere'. But I couldn't understand what horror my daughter had confronted and why I hadn't been able to protect her. Instead of asking her about this, we continued arguing about my relationship with the artist she seemed to detest so much.

'I don't go to his house, it's his studio.'

I knew my interruption would annoy her, but I felt the need to defend myself. Suddenly, my daughter had situated herself in a superior position to my own, and spoke with flat, almost bored assuredness, the way someone who has uncovered an important secret would speak to someone like me, her mother, who hasn't.

'It's not his studio. That's why they won't let him give painting lessons, because they found out he's been telling a bunch of lies. That's also why they told him to remove the painting from the school. You have no idea what's going on. But Dad knows.'

I didn't even try to defend myself from this attack. I wanted to know how far she would go, and why she mentioned Pablo. She waited for me to react. I didn't, and we stood in the hallway looking at the painting for so long that I thought the time had come for me to leave, but then Berta started talking again.

'Now I understand why that man followed me home, why he gave me that picture in the envelope, and why you interviewed him and brought this painting home. And that's why I want us to have an ibis for a pet. I'm like the boy in the story, who can only see things through a lens of horror. That's why there are only ugly things in my life. The psychologist at school told me that's not true, that there are many things in my life, and many of them are beautiful, but that I only focus on the ugly things. She doesn't understand anything. First, she says one thing, then the other. First, she says I have to look at all the good things there are in my life, and then she tells me I have to learn to live with ugly things, because they're important, too. She says that if I'm feeling sad about what's happening to Mario, there's nothing wrong with that, and that I should see sadness as a good thing, because it means that Mario is very important to me and is a part of my life, and that will always be important. And she says you and Dad will always be a part of my life, which is a good thing, too.'

At that point, she looked at me searchingly and shrugged her shoulders, furrowing her brow as if she were waiting for me to clarify this apparent contradiction. But I didn't know what to say. I had the feeling she had already discussed all this with her father.

'Mario and I wanted to see things differently, that's why we trained our eyes and made an effort to learn. If we could see the elements that make up an object separately, reality would be completely different and everything would change. Ugly things would cease to be ugly, and people would have to use different words to explain the world. The way we relate to each other would be different, and it would be possible to have an ibis at home.'

'Why is it so important to have that bird as a pet?'

'I already told you. To keep me company.'

—

At night, before going to bed, I saw that I had an email from Isabel, full of her impatience and concerns and doubts about the actual possibility of publishing the article about Vicente Rojo. I didn't respond. I dreamed again of the magnificent ibis that stalked through the hallway of my home, free of the presence of the painting, and that in its wake it littered the floor with pieces of paper on which Berta had drawn her tiny circles.

There was something theatrical about the declarations of sorrow about Mario's illness that took place at the school. He had been pulled out of classes to undergo a series of tests, and the vast majority of his classmates turned his absence into an almost sacred matter. It was best not to mention it directly, just in case certain words could awaken the latent possibilities. In any case, his illness created an infinite series of codes and alternate language through which they could show, above all, their fear and disbelief. Such messages were difficult to decode for those of us on the outside of that tragic and sorrowful group.

Berta's teacher asked me to meet with her again. I supposed that the main topic of conversation would be Mario and the different strategies the students had come up with to cope with this setback. As far as I knew, nothing like this had happened at the school before. I wasn't wrong. To begin with, the teacher brought me into the strange and sad environment that had overtaken the school. All the students, and all the teachers, too, were having a terrible time with it, but the staff were particularly concerned for Berta, because she was one of those closest to Mario. She said this in a way that made it seem like there was some risk Mario's illness was contagious. She asked me how Berta was behaving at home and showed great surprise when I told her that she was 'normal'.

'What do you mean, normal?'

'The same as always. Have you noticed anything different?'

The teacher furrowed her brow and gave a start as if a shiver had just run down her spine. That's when I realised that this woman and I, who must have been about the same age, had always spoken to each other formally, as if we were complete strangers. This seemed like an important detail. I've never been good at managing the distance that can open up through the use of language and its formalities.

'I've already told you that we're concerned. Especially because of that game she used to play with Mario, the fainting game.'

'Well, I think that game is over now.'

The teacher couldn't hide her concern and discomfort.

'Yes, of course it's over, but perhaps you need to talk to her, because the school psychologist has told us ...'

'I do speak with her,' I interrupted.

'With the psychologist?'

'With Berta. And she also told me what the psychologist thinks of all this. I don't think for one minute that the fainting game caused that boy to fall ill, or my daughter either. They just want to see reality in another way, to see things differently. They're fifteen years old, they don't like what they see and they're trying to see a different world. I don't see anything wrong with that.'

My daughter's teacher was the same age as me, but much skinnier — not a single kilo overweight. She was wearing a casual but well-coordinated outfit: clothes made from high-quality materials, discreet makeup and expensive jewellery. She was still concerned, but she was no longer prepared to tell me how I should talk to my daughter, not now. So I continued talking:

'Do you know who Jusep Torres Campalans is?'

'I beg your pardon?'

'Or Vicente Rojo?'

'I'm sorry, but I don't understand.' Her concern had turned into discomfort. 'Who are you referring to? Are they students here at the school?' I remembered the painter's fury when he had learned that none of the teachers at the school knew who he was, and thought of all the books and catalogues filled with examples of his work sitting on the desk in my study.

'No, *I'm* sorry, I got distracted. Jusep Torres Campalans was a painter from Mollerussa, a friend of Picasso's. He was in Paris at the start of the twentieth century and then he went into exile in Mexico, in Chiapas, which perhaps you might have heard of, thanks to Subcomandante Marcos. That's what I was thinking about. Forgive me, and don't worry about Berta, she'll be fine.'

I decided that the meeting would end there. Right as I was about to say goodbye and leave her office, when it was obvious that neither of us had managed to reassure the other, I asked the teacher about the art lessons the students were supposed to receive. Vicente Rojo's name had clearly meant absolutely nothing to her. Relieved at finally being able to discuss a subject about which she thought she knew everything, she informed me that there would be no painting classes. There had been a setback with the individual who was to be in charge. When they spoke about Mario's illness, they also used the word *setback*. The fact was, the supposed painter who had offered to give painting lessons had deceived them. He wasn't an artist at all; he could barely hold a brush. Fortunately, one of the parents got wind of the sham before anything serious could happen. That was lucky, because the school already had enough problems. The parent who had put Vicente Rojo's name forward for the classes had apologised, because he had been the first one duped. Vicente Rojo had met the parent in an art supply store in the neighbourhood and somehow made him believe he was an artist of certain distinction in Mexico. The story was hardly believable, and the art teacher had been wary from the beginning. Luckily, the whole grotesque episode had come to an end before anything bad could happen.

Prosopagnosia is an illness in which the sufferer can no longer identify faces, whether it be their own or the faces of others. In other words, the sufferer sees a face, but they are unable to associate its features with a particular individual. Some time ago, my daughter learned about this illness at school, in a class where she was taught some introductory psychological concepts. Because of this, and also because her teacher had told her that the brain perceives what the education system teaches it to perceive, my daughter and her friends had begun to play that strange game that became of such great concern to the faculty. To make certain that this illness truly existed, after my second visit to Berta's teacher in a short period of time, and after a good snack in a bar near the school where I thought I saw the artist in the distance, I searched Google for a definition of *prosopagnosia*. The search produced over seven hundred thousand results, although that fact has little meaning beyond the number of times that thousands of people across the world have typed the same word at some point. Then I searched for *Vicente Rojo* and Google produced almost a million online instances in which those words appeared. This was another insignificant fact, because those two words by themselves were so common and had so many different uses that they could be combined for an infinite number of reasons that had nothing to do with the artist. So, the figure itself was as misleading as it was overwhelming. In taking a moment to talk about these search results here, my intention is to consider several indicators that in some circumstances might be of interest, and in others might be misleading. All of which is to say, paying attention to everything isn't always useful.

The most relevant result was that, right there on my computer screen, a seemingly endless series of images appeared. On the one hand, there were reproductions of paintings that were undeniably related to those I had seen in the catalogues the artist had given to me, and on the other, an almost infinite sequence of images of a face, always the same one, but at different ages, in different poses and contexts. A man with very dark eyes, deep rather than sunken, with a gaze that seemed melancholy and unyielding at the same time. Altogether, his broad forehead, straight nose, and well-groomed beard give the effect of a great man, the kind of illustrious figure you might see in a sculpture. That was the first thought that occurred to me. The second was that this image had absolutely nothing to do with the man I had spent hours interviewing. There was a kind of *forced* resemblance, something like imitation: shirt collars poking out of the V-neck sweaters; a beard that was well-trimmed but a little wispier; hand movements that I now realised were affected, and concerned with replicating the careful postures of Vicente Rojo in the photos on the internet. In many of those images, the true artist's hands were visible. It wasn't for nothing that he had written about the vital importance of that part of his body.

Among the images that reproduced the artist's work, I

lingered over one, in which a series of pyramids in brown tones rested on what looked like a watery surface, as if the painting had captured that exact moment when it stops raining and the ground becomes like a mirror. Each of the pyramids had another symmetrical one joined at its base, which meant the landscape doubled and revealed another dimension. In paintings like these, my daughter searches for the new dimensions of reality, the perspective that will reveal the way everything truly functions: the answer to all the mysteries.

I also stopped to look, once more, at the legendary cover that Vicente Rojo had designed for *One Hundred Years of Solitude*. A professor in one of my literature classes had spoken about it. That's probably the only thing I thought about, the first time I googled Vicente Rojo. Before the first interview, when I wanted to know who the Mexican artist was, I typed his name into the search engine. This was before embarking upon a series of interviews that led nowhere. Back then I had been overwhelmed by the quantity of material about the artist that already existed, and I had been dismayed at my own ignorance and my daring at the thought that I could possibly write something about him. This is why I hadn't paid any attention to the face in the photos. I'd had no interest in the face of Vicente Rojo that was offered to me by the internet; I was satisfied with what I'd seen of the man who followed my daughter home one day because she had fainted at school, who gave her a painting and told me his name was Vicente Rojo. I had come down with a clear case of prosopagnosia.

I had to get in touch with Isabel and tell her that the man who thought he was Vicente Rojo was crazy. A fraud, an imposter. The idea that I wouldn't have to write the article for the newspaper was a relief, but it also made me sad. The feeling of having been deceived was much more complicated, and as such, much more difficult to describe. I *could* fall into my habitual state of victimhood and arrive at the conclusion that human beings are toxic to one another, and that there are many ways to destroy the stage upon which other people are supposed to play out their lives. It was much more soothing to conclude that he was crazy, because then there would be no point wasting energy trying to understand his motives, or hoping for an explanation. However, all these days I had spent thinking I had to write the article about the artist had made my job in the communications department of the insurance company much more bearable. That had been because I thought I was finally learning important truths while I was immersed in Vicente Rojo's world, where human beings are linked to the essential material of life. In Vicente Rojo's world, colours, which are nothing more than reflections, can shake our souls and reveal things we don't see at first glance. In his world, it is possible to live alongside intellectuals and geniuses who have different ways of explaining things and can offer us comfort because everything they have learned moves us closer to truth, harmony, and peace. All of this translated into a feeling like satisfaction, the tranquillity that comes from feeling like you are capable of giving shape to tiny events that little by little fill the void. It doesn't matter if it's a bottomless abyss, because the truly transcendental things are the tiny events we create ourselves.

None of this would help me find the right words to explain to Isabel that I wouldn't be turning in an interview or an article or anything about Vicente Rojo. Despite having felt so close to an important revelation, despite almost having grasped the sort of mystical truth that seems capable of transforming a human being, everything was very confused. I had ignored Isabel's calls along with the emails where, for the millionth time, she asked me when I would be able to send her the text. She had said it was a good week to find space for it in the newspaper. It was as if she was addressing herself to a person who wasn't me. Those calls and messages seemed to be for a journalist who was capable of making decisions and working through any setback. I was an insecure, timid, and fat woman, unable even to comfort her own fifteen-year-old daughter, who was going through a traumatic experience.

When Berta arrived home, I asked her to show me how to play prosopagnosia. At first, she didn't understand, because she and her friends must have called it something else. She told me she was very tired, because she had spent the afternoon with Mario. When I asked her how he was, she didn't answer. I've already tried to describe how during those weeks any comment or gesture related to Mario acquired a theatrical patina. It was clear that my daughter's response to her friend's situation was a solemn silence. But she did explain that playing just for the sake of playing didn't work. When they did it, they were training themselves to see things differently. I asked her if she'd achieved her goal. It took her a while to answer, and after a silence that had nothing dramatic about it at all she told me that for her, the ibis wasn't ugly at all. And without waiting for me to respond, she told me how her classmates had decided to paint a mural with Mario's face on the wall of the gym at school. It would be a huge mural, a tribute to Mario from all his classmates.

She had fallen into the sofa, her head resting on a pillow, her eyes closed. I was surprised by what I was seeing, as if we had already started playing prosopagnosia. She had shaved her hair again, and you could the little hairs beginning to emerge from her stubbly scalp. I didn't recognise the huge hoodie she was wearing, and I imagined it must belong to Mario, but I didn't ask her about it.

'The art teacher won't let us paint the mural.'

'Well, I think it sounds like a nice idea.'

She opened her eyes at the sound of my voice, but she wasn't looking at me. She was staring at some fixed, unknown spot. I thought that she had, in fact, learned how to see things differently.

'They're waiting for the final act.'

I was surprised to hear my daughter use the phrase 'final act', another sign of the drama imposed by Mario's illness.

'They say we have to wait, but the art teacher said it's not a good idea to cover a whole wall with graffiti. She doesn't understand anything. She couldn't care less about the students. I bet she's angry because we asked that artist friend of yours to help us.'

At that point she turned her gaze on me, and it felt like she was trying to look at me from the back of her eyes, from the exact point where the optic nerve transmits images to the brain.

'You know he's not my friend, and besides—'

'Daniel says he can do it himself, because he's good at drawing and he's done some cool graffiti already, but I think it's a good idea for a real artist to help us so it doesn't turn out to be a crappy portrait. That's why the art teacher got so angry. They're waiting for the final act and then they want to do something more formal, but we want to paint the mural now, so Mario can see it. We already know that artist guy is crazy, but I bet he can help us, he must know something about painting. If they don't let us, we'll go at night and do it, but then everything will be much more difficult.'

'I met with your teacher this afternoon.'

'I know, Mum, I know. But all you parents have to help us now, because it's really important for all the students, and even more so for Mario. I already told everyone you'd talk to the artist and ask him to help us.'

Berta's gaze had softened again, and she looked at me in the way she had since the truce imposed by her friend's illness. She was demanding once more that I behave like a mother. My voice sounded almost painful.

'Berta, I don't understand. I don't understand anything at all.'

She got up from the sofa and came over to me. She hugged me, and I wasn't sure if she seeking consolation, or offering it.

'I know, Mum. I know. But it doesn't matter.'

Intellectuals have an obligation to denounce abuses of power and every element of society whose purpose is not in line with the struggle towards the collective good. Good artists are considered as such because they place otherwise hidden truths before the eyes of other human beings. The purpose of journalism is to show the population the greatest number of events possible so that we can be aware of just how much is going on in the world we live in. Then we can understand that each and every one of these events affects us directly, some way or another. The intellectual, the artist, and the journalist have a responsibility to the society in which they live. This is a responsibility they cannot shirk. We spent many hours discussing this and other similar themes in my last class at university. I have to say they always seemed like very abstract topics that had little to do with my daily life. On the other hand, there were other students who engaged in the conversation with true fervour. They were convinced that those of us gathered there at the university had, or one day would have, a responsibility to our society. At the end of the day, the State had spent a lot of money building universities and paying professors and lecturers to instruct us on how to build a better nation: one that was more advanced, more supportive, more egalitarian, more cultured, more conscious ... In those discussions, my classmates took each other on, brandishing their enthusiastic idealism at our cynical professors who told us that in a best-case scenario, once we left the university with our degrees, we might find a job in a media outlet where our role would be to replicate messages of power. As for me, I was incapable of joining either side of the argument, simply because I was unable to see that every event happening anywhere in the world was directly related to my life, which I felt was circumscribed with much closer and more immediate boundaries.

I was thinking about all of this on the last afternoon I met up with the man who thought he was Vicente Rojo. It had been very difficult to secure this last interview. For several days, the artist had ignored my calls, and I thought that perhaps he, too, had realised that once his sham was discovered, the best thing would be to blow up any bridges that linked us. He must have been thinking that I knew about his absurd lies, which is why it would be so uncomfortable to have to talk to me, because I'd probably demand an explanation for everything that had happened. All in all, I think I deserved one. When I was about to give up on the idea of talking with him again, Berta asked me to keep trying. In another absurd twist of events, now it was she who needed that man.

Finally, I reached him on the phone. I thought I could detect impatience in his voice. We made no mention of our previous interviews, or of my supposed interest in writing an article about him. I told him I needed to speak to him about something related to my daughter's school. We set a time and place, and that was the end of the conversation. He would meet me two days later, in the late afternoon, in his studio.

It was a gloriously sunny afternoon. I left home a few hours earlier than the time I'd agreed upon with the man who thought he was Vicente Rojo, because I wanted to take a walk and think about what I was going to say. But the only thing I remember is that I spent a lot of time in a café close to his studio. I was going over all the notes that I had taken in our previous meetings. I thought that I truly must not have been as smart as I had thought I was in other moments of my life, or that there must be something seriously wrong with my brain if I had never realised that, throughout all the conversations we held, that man had limited himself to reciting fragments he had memorised from books written by the real Vicente Rojo, especially from his *Open Diary*. It ought to have been very easy to catch on to what was happening. I should never have wasted so much time, I should never have called Isabel to propose working together on something that turned out to be such a nightmare, and I should never have told him so many things about my life. This last point didn't just make me uncomfortable, it made me furious. Having been fooled by his absurd game and giving him access to my most personal thoughts put me in a very disadvantaged position. His idea of me must surely now be as terrible as my own.

I had also been on the cusp of giving Isabel, who was clearly still important to me, good reason to think I was an idiot. If I ended up having to tell her that I couldn't write the article about Vicente Rojo's visit to our city, she'd surely want to know why, and I had no idea how to tell her without making an absolute fool of myself. There was the option of waiting for her to grow tired of my lack of response, letting things slide until the artist's presence was eclipsed by some other piece of news that the paper would consider more interesting. These things happen all the time in the media. All the same, I couldn't let go of my feelings of anxiety, and I had that recurring thought again: a downward spiral that began by disappointing Isabel, a disappointment that kept growing until the whole world knew I was a fake who could never be a journalist, much less an intellectual engaged with society. I didn't even deserve a place in that society, so the only answer was to push me out beyond the borders, out of the world itself. If I didn't send Isabel anything, then at last the ending I had always been waiting for, that I had always felt was so near, would finally arrive. I could be found out at any moment; the abyss had always been right next to me. And if at last the possibility or the illusion of a woman capable of writing an article about Vicente Rojo disappeared completely, everything would stop making sense, because all that would be left would be a fat forty-three-year-old who spends eight hours a day writing and sending out press releases about new insurance policies and who understands nothing. Letting go of the possibility of publishing the article would be like accepting that it is impossible to have an ibis at home.

Perhaps because I was resisting coming to terms with all this, when I was about to leave the café to go to my last interview with the artist who thought he was Vicente Rojo — and I thought I could hear Isabel's raucous cackling and the murmurs of mass disdain that would greet my failure — I managed to hear the musicality of the strong and blinding language with which I had to compose my article about Vicente Rojo. The written lines could indeed form paragraphs as beautiful as the straight lines of his paintings that depicted the rain over Mexico.

The night before my last interview with the artist, I had dreamt that I was in a large room in a charming house decorated with rugs, books, artworks, and sophisticated handicrafts full of beauty and ancient messages. You entered the room I was in through various doors placed asymmetrically on the walls, which indicated the existence of a great many other rooms. You could also intuit the existence of a sunny patio that, without a doubt, would be one of the major attractions of this house, which was situated in the upscale Mexican neighbourhood of Coyoacán. In my dream I knew all of this because it was not my first time here. On many previous occasions I had attended this literary salon with Fernando Benítez, Federico Álvarez, Carlos Monsiváis, Max Aub, Juan García Ponce, Sergio Pitol, Enrique Vila-Matas, José María Espinasa, Chico Magaña, Pedro Serrano, Jusep Torres Campalans, Juan Antonio Masoliver when he travelled from London, and Bárbara Jacobs when her obligations at the Hotel Poe permitted her. While I write this, I feel I should describe my presence there like Alice's in Wonderland. The person I was in this dream moved about with the same strange familiarity and assuredness as Alice Liddell in the outlandish scenarios she found herself in. Despite all this, I clearly remember how García Ponce was arguing with Torres Campalans about the importance of abstract art. The painter from Mollerussa made gestures of arrogant impatience while his interlocutor repeated for the thousandth time how abstract art gives form to the invisible, about how artists drift from reality, paradoxically, to immerse themselves in it, to search for what is not in plain sight and give shape to it. Torres Campalans interrupted him and said that the only interesting abstract art is the work made by his friend Pablo, and that all other painters, following the failure of cubism, should spare us their arrogant rubbish. With his measured but firm voice, Vicente Rojo came to the defence of abstract art. He didn't want to annoy Jusep Torres Campalans, but he also didn't want to let the conversation slide into the absurd and impossible tangents that so delight the Catalan painter. If things kept on that way, Max Aub would end up insisting on some kind of word game that would put an end to all conversation. This is why Vicente Rojo said that Mexican muralism provided great works of art that are essential to all human beings, but that doesn't mean, by any account, that it was the only valid form of art from Mexico. There were many abstract artists whose work has helped the thought and culture of Mexico and the world move forward. Masoliver took advantage of a pause from Vicente Rojo to say that although he was tremendously bored by this debate about the importance of realist and abstract art, surrealist or symbolic art, James Joyce was a realist, despite the fact that there have been so many absurd theories written about his work. Realism is very limited, Masoliver repeated several times, the function of art cannot only be to faithfully reproduce what we see, above all because what we see is barely ever interesting enough to be reproduced infinitely. This is why he was defending Joyce's realism. Obviously, Joyce was writing about a real Ireland, the Dublin he knew so well and where he suffered so much, but he didn't limit himself to reproducing what he saw. Masoliver's voice grew deeper and stronger when someone, maybe it was Bárbara Jacobs, said that the Anglo-Saxon literary tradition is very realist.

It's not just that, he said, but as readers, Anglo-Saxons aren't at all prepared for literature that is abstract or intellectual. Masoliver begged his fellow guests not to talk about metaliterature. Enrique Vila-Matas said that metaliterature, like autofiction, does not exist; a comment that Chema Espinasa celebrated with raucous applause, while he asked to speak about exile, because he still had a lot to say about his grandfather, who was a Republican mayor in a little town near Barcelona, in Montcada i Reixac. But then Chema Espinasa contradicted himself and said that he'd rather talk about poetry, which was seconded by Chico Magaña, who had left a few copies of the latest book published by his delightful press, Monte Carmelo, on the table. They caught the eye of several of the salon members, like Sergio Pitol, who caressed the cover elegantly before opening the book. Pedro Serrano came over to admire the book's beauty as well, and then mentioned an article he'd published in his journal *Cartapacios* about Magaña's editions. In the dream I felt that some of the words being said were addressed to me, and it was my turn to say something. My voice came out clearly, without trembling. It was my turn to participate in the salon and my fellow guests looked at me with interest. So, I gave my speech, in language that was absolutely impossible to understand. I spoke like those characters in Charlie Chaplin films who make noises that sound like they might be words. In my dream, no one realised that even though my speech carried on for a long time, I never spoke a single world. No one, not even me.

I kept on talking calmly in my incomprehensible language until a gust of wind opened one of the doors to the room to reveal the huge patio, filled with palms trees and plants and other shrubs whose names I didn't know. Through the door came a huge, majestic ibis. In the same way no one had seemed to notice my absurd language, no one seemed surprised to see this enormous bird stalking around the elegant room, without interrupting the literary salon. The ibis belonged in these surroundings, and what's more, its entrance revealed the presence of many more ibises on the patio. I didn't need to see them to know it was true. In the same way that such conversations were possible in this dream house, so was the peaceful presence of these birds. The ibises, like me, had arrived at a place where they were no longer in danger.

After briefly watching the majestic parade of the bird amongst the salon attendees, I continued prattling while Bárbara Jacobs took my hand and looked at me with compassion. She told me that it was all over: everyone had left. There was no reason to keep crying, because she had understood everything. There was no need to run away anymore, and I didn't have to leave, because I could stay right here, in her Hotel Poe.

Nothing led me to believe that the afternoon's visit, which would be my last one, would be any different to the others in which we had discussed his childhood, literary salons in Mexico, or his work. Like on previous occasions, he was holding a pencil in his right hand. It made me think that in thrillers, they often discover the murderer's identity because of little details like this. But then I remembered that I wasn't as smart as I thought I was.

He invited me to sit at the same table as always, in the wicker chairs so carefully set out. The studio was as clean as it had been on all my other visits, but I was able to discern something different. On one of the shelves where I had seen the canvasses lined up as if they were books, there was an empty space that allowed me to catch sight of the perfectly blank canvas of one of the paintings that, at one point, I had imagined to be covered with the brushstrokes and oil paints of the artist. What's more, another one of those pristine canvasses was sitting on the table, with a brand-new pencil resting on top of it. Once I noticed it, I couldn't help but find it ridiculous, even if it revealed the true attitude of the supposed artist.

The unused pencil brought to mind one of the many books about Vicente Rojo that I had been consulting over the past few days, *The Pencil's Apology*. It was another gem of a book that collects the artist's work, but this time it came with a sensitive and razor-sharp text by the surgeon Arnoldo Kraus. In the book, Kraus investigates his fascination with pencils, especially the ones that, through use, have ended up short and worn down, the ones he never throws away and keeps in an old cigar box. When you hold the book in your hands, it's difficult to put it down again, just like with certain pencils, as if we wished to be ready at all times for the moment these objects decide to manifest themselves and reveal the messages they surely are hiding.

My meeting with the man passing himself off as Vicente Rojo seemed like an awful reproduction, a ridiculously pretentious and worthless copy of the collaborations and relationships evidenced by so many valuable books and catalogues. I felt like I was watching a child's game in which two participants imitate their parents, or actors they see on television. I had played these sorts of games all the time at school.

He began the conversation:

'Why did you want to see me again?'

'Lately there has been a lot going on at my daughter's school.'

He grew tense, and with a violent gesture he gripped his pencil so tightly his fingers went white. Why didn't he remember that Vicente Rojo was left-handed, that he had hated school because they used to tie back his left hand? By becoming right-handed, why was he conceding victory to the people who had done something so insensitive? His eyes were shinier than when he had opened the door, and he was clearly making an effort to hold my gaze. After the slightest of pauses, during which I might have tried to test him, I went on.

'Perhaps you've heard that one of my daughter's best friends is very ill?'

He kept on gripping the pencil and it seemed like his cheeks were flushed beneath his beard.

'Yes, I heard about it. Unfortunately, you know how news like this gets around. But you also know I have nothing to do with the school.'

At that moment I thought that maybe he was the one testing me out, trying to get me to reveal how much I knew about his lies. That moment also made me think of thriller movies, and of the fact that I wasn't very smart.

'It's Mario. He's got cancer, and all his classmates, well, I'd say all of the students really, are very affected. You know how impressionable kids are at that age — everything is much more traumatic,' I said, blushing. 'My daughter, for example, has been much sadder and more vulnerable since she found out.' It seemed like the tension in his hands was subsiding. 'I guess they're afraid, and they want to do something with all these feelings they have. They've decided to paint a mural with Mario's portrait on one of the walls at school. And they want you to help them. Could you?'

I saw a tired old man sitting before me. I was asking him to help a bunch of teenagers with some graffiti. I tried to decide how best to progress from a moment like this. Perhaps I was waiting for the man passing himself off as Vicente Rojo to begin one of those long speeches I had yearned for on previous afternoons, the ones that ended up enthralling me. I wasn't able to steer the conversations, as could be seen by the silence we had become immersed in for a long time. In the end, he chose to speak, and when I failed to reply, he kept going.

'If what you are doing weren't so crazy, I'd think it was very cruel.'

Despite everything I knew, I was hoping that this whole matter would find its logic, the missing piece of the puzzle that would put everything in place and allow us to find a reasonable explanation for what was going on. I was waiting for the magic words that would make everything comprehensible, and they could only come from him.

'I don't understand what you're saying. Have you really come here to ask me to help your daughter's friends paint a mural of a kid who has cancer?'

I sat there without responding, avoiding looking him in the eyes. I remembered arguments with Pablo in which he had reproached me for my inability to perceive the pain I could cause others. More than once he'd accused me of being irresponsibly cruel, but I'd always felt his accusations were mostly the result of his poor command of language. Pablo had no reason to accuse me of being cruel. In all likelihood he was accusing me of something else, but I never quite understood what. In the end, he was the one who abandoned me and Berta.

'I think it's a good idea. We can help these kids out. We'll paint the portrait of their sick classmate, you'll get your article, and your daughter will get her disgusting bird.'

I had to remind myself that on this particular afternoon, I was the one with the moral high-ground. That old man was just a ridiculous fraud. He had tried to pass himself off as one of Mexico's most prestigious contemporary artists. Who did he think he would fool? Even my daughter, who was only fifteen years old, had tried to warn me. She had warned me with the same desperation she used later to ask me to get the man to help her with the mural. In my dream, Vicente Rojo had complained that muralism continues to be considered the most significant Mexican art form. With anger, he remembered this quote from David Alfaro Siqueiros: 'There's no other way but ours', and how all the young artists who were being called *the breakaways* — he was one of them — had wanted to show how wrong that statement was. It was all so feverish.

I asked him if he was refusing to do the portrait because he was against muralism. He looked at me wide-eyed, breathed in, and cleared his throat.

'I don't know what you're angling for, but neither you nor any of the arrogant teachers at that school will get to me to renounce this life that has cost me so much to build. Leave me in peace.' He cleared his throat again. 'I've never said I'm against muralism. How could I be? I just said that I'm annoyed by *the idea that abstract artwork is impossible if that artwork is Mexican, and that theories that are rooted in the darkest moments of our history and opposed to modernity continue to hold sway.'*

In the silence that followed I took out the copy of *Open Diary* he himself had given me. It didn't take me long to find the quote, which he had underlined. I showed it to him.

'So, have you read it?'

I nodded.

'In that case you have plenty of material for your article. That's what you wanted, wasn't it?'

'I'm afraid not. I'm very confused. Are you going to help the kids paint the mural? I don't want to talk about my article, I just came because my daughter wanted me to ask for your help.'

'And I told you I would. That should be enough, shouldn't it?'

On the surface, yes, that was enough. But I felt like I couldn't move.

'Why did you offer to teach a class at the school?'

'I think we discussed this before. Today you haven't got your tape recorder on the table, so I imagine that what we're talking about now is unrelated to your article, or your essay, or whatever it is you're writing. I met a representative from the parents' committee, and when I told him about my work, he thought it would be interesting if I gave a class for the students. Believe me, I've come out of this mess looking as bad as anyone, even as bad as you.'

Once again, he reminded me of Pablo, and I was irritated by the way he was speaking to me. 'Well, I never tried to make anyone believe I'm a famous painter,' I said.

'Are you sure?'

Ever since I walked into his studio that afternoon, he had been deploying a manipulative strategy to confuse me. He offered brief and painful confessions, on the one hand, with affirmations that seemed to perpetuate his little farce on the other. In any case, he had achieved his goal of bewildering me. Now, as I write this, I realise how many times I've had to describe myself as bewildered, confused, or disconcerted in this story. Be that as it may, I think that at some point I tried to move the conversation away from such unstable terrain, even if it was very difficult for me. When at last I thought he was going to accept the situation and put together a reasonable explanation, he focused all his cruelty on me and everything fell apart. I didn't know how to answer his questions. After I stayed silent for long enough that he realised I wasn't going to respond, he continued:

'Are you sure you haven't been trying to pass yourself off

as someone completely different from who you truly are? Now we're getting somewhere interesting. We're getting closer to an essential and enthralling topic: truth and lies.'

"It's a very complicated topic. There are millions of books about it. But will you be able to tell me the difference between truth and lies?'

"Are you interviewing me again? Which question do you want me to respond to first?'

I had no interest in listening to a crazy man's discourse on such an essential topic. If the man who made people call him Vicente Rojo could establish a hypothesis, I would believe it, and from there I would create my own subsequent discourse that would act like a beacon of thought for me for a period of time. When it came down to it, at one point I was trying to write an essay on Vicente Rojo that was supposed to be some kind of intellectual and moral guide. I was ready to nail down the words and thoughts of this man to turn them into an instruction manual you could consult in moments of anxiety and confusion, like on those mornings when I found it impossible to get out of bed because there was nothing stimulating in anything I was doing. After Pablo left, everything was like a giant blank page or empty canvas that I was supposed to fill, even though I had no idea how.

I was thinking about all this while the fake painter kept on talking. Like the speech I had given in my dream, there were moments when I was actually able to follow his rant. It hardly mattered to him if I was listening or not. He was making a distinction between reality and truth. I had read something similar recently in an article. Perhaps he had read it, too. We accept as real whatever is tangible, what we can perceive through one of our senses, but truth is something that contains some sort of essential knowledge that brings us closer to the materials we are made of. Everything he was saying struck me as acceptable parts of a discourse that I was beginning to recognise, the famous puzzle pieces that fit together to form a meaningful image.

But I still felt a sort of pang that let me know I shouldn't accept this man's ideas. He was a fraud. That crazy man who had tried to pass himself off as Vicente Rojo said that the only meaning of existence is searching for truth and mistrusting reality. Because ultimately, reality was something built for us by others. At one point he began talking about me, or at least I think he did. He was talking about timid people who are too scared to search for their own truth and make do with a comfortable reality. But that wasn't enough. He asked me something he'd asked many times before in our previous meetings: *why is publishing this article about me so important to you?* I would have liked to have told him that he was mistaken — that it wasn't him I wanted to write about, but the real Vicente Rojo and his work — but I didn't dare. Because I was still incapable of interrupting his speech, he then asked me what lies *I* had told. I should have told him that I always tried to be honest with everyone, especially myself. That was a tired old line, a cliché. I could have said it, even if I had to say it in my Chaplinesque language, because our conversation was unfolding much like the literary salon in my dream, even if we were meeting outside of the elegant room in the charming house in Coyoacán.

The questions without answers kept on coming, questions like 'What is your truth?' until finally the answers came, too, but still from his mouth. He said that I had appeared in his studio one afternoon like Alice down the rabbit hole. I was caught off-guard by the reference to Lewis Carroll, which I myself had thought of while interpreting my dream about the intellectuals in Mexico, but then I remembered that this man knew almost all of Vicente Rojo's *Open Diary* by heart, and there are many references to the girl who steps through the looking glass. This was the degree to which this fraud in front of me had been able to manipulate my thoughts.

He said that I had arrived at his studio asking him to tell his story, not *his truth*, and that I was begging for *my own truth*. It hadn't escaped his attention that it was thanks to him that my fantasy of being a bright and cultured journalist who knows a good story when she sees one had come true. We had used each other; each of us had played at what we most wanted to be. Or, in other words, I had used his game to start playing my own. Now though, I'm not sure if that's what he said or what I thought. Like Alice, I had been searching for a way to make reality function differently, like how in Looking-Glass World you have to jog slowly to move forward quickly, or how the fastest route to a house you want to enter is by walking away from it. This search united us. He was happy to be my Mad Hatter and guide me through a world where everything works backwards. Vicente Rojo is left-handed, like Lewis Carroll, whose real name wasn't Lewis Carroll but Charles Lutwidge Dodgson. He was never in line with the social conventions of his time either. This is why the fake artist had tried to pretend he was left-handed, even though he never managed to pull it off.

According to the fake artist, it wasn't a matter of Berta searching for a world in which it was possible to have an ibis at home, or inventing games to try to see the world differently. It was all about me, and how I was asking my daughter for the same thing I had been looking for at his studio: I wanted someone to narrate the world in a different way, in a way where we all fit in. According to him, there was nothing coincidental at all about the fact that the three of us (me, him, and Berta) had all arrived at the same point.

He was also searching for a world where the rules worked backwards. At least I think that's what he meant. He began talking about Lilith, Adam's first wife, and the world that she had constructed. He didn't think it was true that she would have ended up surrounded by devils and seducing men while they slept. That was a story put together to disparage her, to negate any possibility of the existence of an alternative. If someone asked what had become of the first woman who had dared to defy God, the best option was to invent a terrible ending for her so no one else would try it. But he knew that Lilith's ending was far from dark. He even went so far as to say that the Paradise designed by her and her children wasn't enough, that she didn't agree with all the rules they were trying to force on her to ensure her safety and that of her children. She renounced Paradise and God's rule. And, in the opinion of the man who thought he was Vicente Rojo, such an exercise in valour could never have such a dreadful ending. Lilith's children must be living out there somewhere, free of the rules and obligations of a tyrannical God, capable of building a world run by different rules, where everyone can find their place and they can live according to their own truths in a Paradise that is unconditional, free of artifice.

The fake artist discovered that he would have liked to have been Vicente Rojo one afternoon when he was working in an art supply store, and he overheard someone talking about a Mexican artist who had a fascinating body of work and no enemies. This last detail was what most caught his attention, so he tried to remember the name until it became a part of him. He told me he could recount the story of an everyday life, one where nothing happened for many years. There are many lives like that, of which there is little to say. But if I preferred, he could also tell me a horrible story, full of yearning and insatiable hunger, of violence, blood, pain, and punishment. He said that in the end, every story comes down to the same thing: human beings and their feelings. I could have chosen the story he would tell me, but I sat motionless, I knew his questions weren't intended to draw me into the conversation, but were merely a preamble for him to finally tell me the story of the man who thought he was Vicente Rojo. I was ready for anything. I knew that when a discourse establishes the conditions of reality, it becomes an act of violence that imposes itself over all others.

He told me the story of a misunderstanding that, if you listened to it carefully, might seem funny. It was the story of a man who felt one day that he could no longer keep living the life he had led for many years, so he decided to leap into the void, leaving behind the fog in which he existed to do something important. He communicated this to those he was closest to. He told everyone that he was ready to take the plunge. Obviously, the decision surprised his wife, his children, and his relatives, along with the few friends he still had at this stage of his life. Without a doubt, it was the juiciest piece of gossip in his circle, and everyone wondered what this great leap forward would be. When would it happen? How would he protect himself? What would happen to his wife (his children already had their own lives, and had distanced themselves from their father), and where would he jump from?

The fact of the matter is, people were thinking and gossiping about his great leap more than he was. Before he could realise what was happening, the stage had been set for him. If it was going to be a great leap, it had to be from the steeple of the church, which was the highest point of the town where he lived. This is when the parish rector got involved, because he had to figure out the best time so that the normal functioning of the church wouldn't be affected, while still allowing for the maximum number of parishioners to observe the repentant man's leap. And so, that man who was so disgusted by his own life never even had the opportunity to explain what this great leap he had planned for himself was, because his whole community had already prepared for what they had understood as the only possible expression of his desire. Early one Sunday, the disgusted man found himself atop the steeple in his town's church, asking himself if he should jump or not. Obviously, no one had thought about what might happen after he jumped, which is to say, during the fall.

If possible, the story about the disgusted man bewildered me even more. The painter who had gone by the name of Vicente Rojo asked me if I thought the man ought to have met the expectations of the others, or if, on the other hand, the only option left was to invent a new life, to believe it was possible to become someone else for whom the men and women in his circle would not prepare a spectacular leap into the void when he spoke of his desire to move forward, to move beyond the things he had known.

In any case, he decided to become Vicente Rojo because he had heard that he was a man with no enemies, and that everyone admired and respected his work. Later on, when he began to research him, he learnt many more details: Vicente Rojo was a painter who wanted to fill a void, a person searching for elemental forms and essential material, the truth we are made up of. Over a long period of time, he searched for all the books, articles, and catalogues he could find to get to know the artist's body of work. One day, he learnt that Vicente Rojo would be visiting the city of his birth, Barcelona, in order to open a big show. He went to the show and did everything he could to meet the artist. By then, it had been quite some time since he abandoned his family and the circle of friends who had so carefully prepared for his leap into the void.

When he heard Vicente Rojo speak and saw his paintings on the Paseo de San Juan, he decided he could no longer move to Mexico — a goal that in his deepest desires, he never quite renounced — and that he should live as close as possible to that street. He would climb to the Paseo's highest point, hoping to see on the horizon the same ship that Vicente Rojo had seen, from that very same place, when he was a boy. He became so obsessed with the artist's paintings that he began to believe that the only place he wanted to live was inside the artist's world. If by just looking at his paintings you could feel like you melted into its forms and became a part of the balance and peace of their composition, it was because the paintings' creator had reached a higher state of knowledge, from which it was possible to remove suffering. His world was full of serenity and equilibrium. Through the geometric forms of his paintings, he had found a better order for things, and made reality better than what it actually was.

That afternoon he gave me his final gift: he spoke to me about the importance of looking at things differently in order to see truth. He said — although I think I also read it in an article about the Mexican artist — that he had undergone a long apprenticeship before he knew how to look at his own paintings and to understand what he was looking for. We mustn't let ourselves be deceived by the number of stimuli our senses can perceive. This principle can be found in the work of the very first philosophers, who tried to build a discourse to explain human behaviour. The most important thing is to find one's own truth: it's a search that never ends, but takes shape as we undertake it. This is why he was drawn to the way Berta looked at his painting when he saw her for the first time at her school.

I wanted to ask him to show me how to look, but I didn't have the courage. Perhaps it wasn't that I needed to write the sentences with which I could reconstruct the thinking and morality of Vicente Rojo, but that I needed something new to focus on, to rid these words of their superficial meanings in order to understand their truth. I could view that man as a fraud who had tried to pass himself off as an important artist, seeking who knows what benefit, or I could see him as an individual who had been brave enough to take his search for meaning to such an extreme that when I met him, he believed he was someone else. I could see myself as an obese woman who had been abandoned by her husband, who is overwhelmed by her daughter's sadness, and who hides away because everything frightens her, or I could see myself as a woman smart enough to make the most of her desire to discover new narratives that make the world bigger, and who works towards finding her own little corner where she can feel comfortable and where things aren't so terrible. Once you stumble across your desired image, you have to defend your narrative at all costs. I had to be strong enough to fend off any negative thoughts that contradicted the image I wanted to see. From this moment on, every piece of the puzzle would fit and my landscape would be filled with geometric figures that come together to form a beautiful melody that explains everything with joy. There would be no words or shadows to fear.

By the time I left his studio, the man who thought he was Vicente Rojo had given me his solemn promise that he would help my daughter's friends paint the portrait of Mario. I never spoke to him again, and Berta never told me if he held true to his word. The teachers never gave the students permission to paint the mural in the gymnasium, but they were allowed to paint one of the walls in the classroom.

I've seen Berta many times standing in front of the painting given to me by the man who thought he was Vicente Rojo. The frame is still broken; we never repaired it. I think that huge, imperfect canvas, which is such a poor copy of the Mexican artist's work, and the painting he gave my daughter, are the only two artworks made by the man I interviewed so terribly, so many times. Perhaps they have no merit besides the fact that they are material proof of a leap into the void: he dared to create something, he dared to show that, despite the perfect story he had built around his identity, his work was not the work of Vicente Rojo. This show of bravery alone made me think he was admirable. Berta was right when she said that keeping that painting in our home was as strange as adopting an ibis.

I kept reading and taking notes about Vicente Rojo while Isabel kept asking for my article about the classes given by a famous Mexican artist in a neighbourhood high school. They had already settled on a publication date.

—

In one of the texts collected in *Open Diary*, Vicente Rojo introduces the writer Max Aub as if he were a character invented by the Catalan painter Jusep Torres Campalans. When I read it, I was impressed by the profound complicity that existed between those two artists. It wasn't just a game of masks and winks, it was a pact between two intellectuals who agreed to dive into a deeper dimension — or a higher dimension, if you prefer — than reality. What we perceive through our senses is not enough; truth is forged in our minds, through intelligence, knowledge, and imagination: so goes the thinking of Vicente Rojo and Max Aub. It's the same thing as when Fernando Pessoa said he had no need to leave his squalid bedroom to travel the world.

I had read in an academic article that Max Aub played a similar game to Pessoa when he published a review of a play that was never performed. The theatre, script, actors, and director never existed either. Without knowing of Aub's precedent, Juan Antonio Masoliver, so Mexican in some ways and such an exile in others, had also published a review of a book that had never been written, by an author and publisher whose absurd names he had invented for the occasion. Another example that springs to mind is a dialogue between two characters, named Vicente and Rojo, with which Marco Perilli opens one of those delightful books about the artist's oeuvre that was lent to me by the man who was convinced he was Vicente Rojo. Perhaps because all of this was swirling around in my mind, I started behaving like I was in my dream, in an elegant room in Coyoacán, at a literary salon full of intellectuals where I had decided I would write an article about Vicente Rojo that would be published by the newspaper in the capital city of the region where I lived. They had already settled on a publication date.

Sure enough, I sent my article to Isabel. Just as she had suggested, I wrote about the experience of twenty or so students from a neighbourhood high school who, unbeknown to them, had attended a painting class given by a very prestigious artist. I described how the initial discomfort of the painter at having to perform publicly slowly became a kind of cryptic complicity with the teenagers, who never stopped asking him about when he painted, how he decided on forms, if he preferred Catalan or Mexican food, if it was really as dangerous to live in Mexico as they said on the news, about why he didn't have a Mexican accent when he spoke, about why he liked Mexico better than Spain, if he had been friends with Frida Kahlo, and if he would help them paint a mural with a portrait of one of their classmates, who was very sick.

I think that in the article I managed to capture the artist's character, the calm he radiated with his voice, and the balance he imposed with each movement of his hands, no matter how small. I created a Vicente Rojo who possessed an important secret, who seemed like some kind of shaman or oracle. Obviously, I made it abundantly clear that his story was an example of hard work. The teenagers who attended this legendary class had to understand the importance of work and the desire to overcome. Thanks to his dedication, a young man from a family deeply affected by war had been able to become one of the most important artists and intellectuals of his time.

I'm not sure I emphasised enough the importance of his contributions to Mexican culture, because I didn't want to harp on how under-educated the teachers at the school must have been, seeing as they had no idea who Vicente Rojo was. Of course, I included the poignant scene of the sisters' piano hanging out the window of an apartment building in Barcelona. Few people can create such a perfect anecdote for explaining how the only world a person has known can collapse in a single moment. It becomes a much crueller image because the collapse is witnessed by a seven-year-old boy. To round out the article, I described the image of the artist amongst the students, standing in front of a wall where they were painting the portrait of a sick classmate.

When I finished writing the article, I asked Berta to read it. In doing that, I realised how important whatever she might have to say would be to me, and then I realised that the simple fact that she would read it had made the whole enterprise worthwhile. Before, the moment when I turned in an article was the moment when all my fears and anxieties appeared. I worried I had got a fact wrong or misinterpreted something, that I had misunderstood an answer from someone I had interviewed, that I'd made a spelling mistake or included something that might offend someone ... In short, I always felt like I'd committed an act of arrogance that would be rightly punished through a sense of generalised disdain. This is why when the article was finally published, I hoped that it would slip by unnoticed and be quickly forgotten.

Berta read my article about Vicente Rojo's classes at her school. She smiled and said she liked it very much. Although she didn't understand a word of it, she thought it was beautiful. She wanted a copy she could keep. She offered no other comment, and for me it was enough that she said she found it beautiful.

Isabel let me know she received the article, but I haven't heard from her since. I've promised myself I won't think about it until the publication date. When that day comes, I plan to celebrate with a huge banquet for me and Berta at home. We might invite one more guest to dine with us; perhaps the man who thought he was Vicente Rojo.